Shadows That Play

GITTE TAMAR

BTW LLC

To those who live behind their fears, you must relinquish your reliance on your peers; only then will you be able to accomplish the full potential of your future years.

Acknowledgments

Hello to all,

Thank you to every last one of you, no matter if your part was big or small.

Thank you to each of my family and friends, you already know who you are, so I will refrain from listing each of your specific names. Just know I will forever be thankful for each one of you who provided me with never-ending troves of love and emotional support.

Thank you to all of my readers for continuing to embark on this journey with me. I am forever indebted to you.

Sincerely,

Contents

Chapter 1

MOMMY?

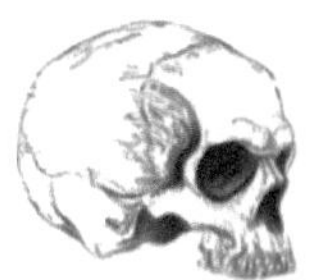

19th Century, England

Rain falls against the hard surface of the uneven cobblestone streets. A woman rushes through a dimly lit alleyway, her arms tightly wrapped around an infant's limp body. A black hood covers her head and shields her eyes, and her hands use the bottom of the cloak to conceal the child. Her paranoia escalates as her steps quicken, and her eyes dart, erratically glancing toward every rippling puddle. Heavy footsteps echo deliberately behind her. The frightened creature's head snaps up to lay eyes on what follows, but nothing is there.

Shadows form from the dimly lit light posts, and the flickering flames cause them to dance. The woman lowers her head, casting her gaze directly at the ground to avoid catching sight of the dark, frolicking observers.

The footsteps behind her transform into a soft run.

At the sound, her torso stiffens, and her jaw tightens. She senses the shadows closing in on her. "Leave my baby alone," she says. "It's not yours; it's mine. *He* is mine."

She glances at the small body wrapped underneath her cloak. Still concealing the baby's identity, she lifts the bundled child to her racing heart and touches his icy skin against hers. She uses her gripping hands to bounce him with a disjointed rhythm as she continues to run while whispering in a soft singing tune to soothe his ears. "Hush, little baby. Don't make a peep. Please, dear Lord, continue to sleep. Your mother's knees are weak, and if she falls, the sound of collapse will usher them all, gnashing and clawing at our tearful crawl. They will drag us to the depths of hell and rip you away from my breast, where forever I want you to stay."

The alleyway tapers, condensing the shadows lurking deep in the void, forcing the darkness to infringe on their imagined sanctuary.

As she senses a presence coming over the top of her hood, her demeanor shifts, and her feet stop beneath her. Whispers clamber as they build in intensity, echoing from every direction, bouncing off every brick in the walls.

Rather than succumb to insanity, however, she takes a deep breath and lifts her head. She has reached a dead end crafted of three dark-stained brick-and-mortar walls running from the filthy cobblestone to the darkened sky.

The motion of her head causes the hood to fall from her skull, revealing her elongated face and protruding high-set cheekbones. Each iris around her pupils is the shade of golden honey. The wind-abraded skin surrounding her lids is puffy from bouts of insomnia, while the whites of her eyes are the color of cream with webs of scarlet veins. Her peeling skin mimics a melting candle as it disintegrates in the harsh, chafing elements. While her hair's dark waves contrast with her pale skin, emphasizing her unwell complexion, the cartilage of her trachea protrudes like a forward-facing spinal cord as her chin tilts toward the sky.

She closes her eyes, and the whispers stop. The footsteps that followed her earlier resume in the distance, gradually growing louder as they approach.

Her eyes spring open, and her gaping mouth shows her unkempt teeth. The revival of the stalking presence makes her release a sound only the underworld can decipher. "You have come to steal him away from me, haven't you?" she asks. She takes a moment to listen for a response and flinches at the sound of the heavy footsteps, clinging tightly to the child. "He's mine. You can't have him!"

The approaching sounds stop. A burst of deep laughter that echoes from the blackest point of the alley cuts the silence short. She recognizes the voice, and the timbre causes her arms to tremble. Her head lowers to address the entity terrorizing her.

A figure steps from the shadows wearing a devious grin. It is Daniel Manley, the child's father. His black coattails hang perfectly pressed, and the brim of his top hat rests meticulously straight, framing his piercing eyes. It's as though his impeccable features have remained flawlessly preserved. He swings his gold-laden walking stick like a pendulum.

His presence terrifies her, causing her to stammer. "I-I thought you were dead," she says, stepping back and holding the child tighter.

Her fear gives him a euphoric high, and he displays each pearly-white tooth as he smiles. He holds the cane in front of him like an extension of his arm and grazes her cheek with its tip. The touch of the cold metal makes her cringe.

Daniel purses his lips. "Do you honestly think I'd leave you alone with my child?" His lungs release a boisterous laugh as he moves the end of the stick underneath her jaw and taps the bottom of her chin. "That may well be the gravest mistake I could ever make. Not to mention, you resemble shit—that alone makes such a decision uncon-scionable. What might people think?"

She recoils her head and spits at him. He finds her rebuttal amusing. "Glad you are still a feisty little creature," he says, stepping toward her. He retracts his cane to his side, and his lips twist to make a saddened face. "That is why it will make getting rid of you so much harder. I've always enjoyed our little banters," he reminisces. "Well, you know what they say: all good things must end."

Her pupils dilate; she's not ready to die. "You can't; you need me. I'm his mouthpiece," she says, shaking the child under the cloak.

Daniel's face can no longer hold its composure, and her statement causes him to cackle with laughter. "Bloody hell, he has nothing to say. You killed him, and everyone knows good mothers don't kill their children."

Agonizingly, her chin lowers, and her eyes stare down at the bulge beneath her cloak. Frantically shaking her head, she scrambles for words. "No, I didn't. He's chipper as the day he was born," she says, wiggling the infant.

Peering down at her, Daniel takes a moment of pause, his eyes skeptical. "Then uncloak him for all to see," he says. As he waits for her response, his lips twitch with a smirk.

Her body squirms as she neurotically rocks the tiny body. "That's preposterous. I will surely wake him," she says.

His face twinges at her defiance, and hatred fills his eyes. His pupils turn an underlying hue of red. His back molars press against one another, and he speaks through clenched teeth. "Reveal him!" he demands.

"You can't have him," she hisses, taking a step back.

With a shrug, he releases his tension and lifts his leather-gloved hand to motion to the shadows. "You hear that, Father? The woman declares I cannot have what is owed to me." The dimensions of his smirk intensify, and his chastising glance silently belittles her. "I contemplated making your death less torturous, but with your reckless behavior, he wins. You will suffer."

Her eyes watch his demeanor shift, and his limbs elongate like those of a stick figure. As his features disappear into an unrecognizable twist, the whispers begin again, reverberating like a million conversations. His body stops its stretching at ten feet tall, and he lingers over her with his featureless face.

The unnaturalness of the elongated sight causes her to panic. She has no choice but to run. Her head snaps in the opposite direction, and her feet speed up to flee, but only a few steps into her departure, an unseen force shoves her frail body from behind, knocking her to the ground.

A bleak, muddy puddle of rainwater mixed with human excrement greets her fall. The foul-smelling substance splashes onto her cheek, and where it lands, open sores form. As each gruesome boil bubbles through her skin, the excruciating pain causes her to release a guttural howl.

Her hand dabs the wounds to assess the damage, and she clutches the baby tighter in her arms to ease her angst over its severity. As her flesh disintegrates, she tilts her head down to prevent the rain from entering the open wounds and catches sight of her blurry reflection in the discolored water. Every bit of repugnance buried deep inside reflects on her face. There is no escape.

Thunder sounds from overhead like grotesque laughter heckling her hideous exterior.

Her eyes water profusely with terror, and her tears add to the putrid liquid beneath her. "I'm his mother; you can't take him," she says. She frenetically rocks the child to keep him from crying as her eyes dart around to see if Daniel is nearby. Not seeing him, she holds the bundle with one hand and removes the opposite hand from underneath the soaked black cloak. Her scabbed knuckles and yellow-tinged nails reach toward the cloth covering the baby.

The anticipation of the child's unwrapping provokes the storm above, and as the thunder growls, it fills the air with booming condemnation.

Peeling back the last piece of damp fabric concealing the child's head brings a sensation of undying love to her fluttering heart. She doesn't distinguish its decomposing state as she gazes upon the child's lifeless blue skin; instead, she perceives a soul untainted by death.

Removing the cloak, she places it on the wet cobblestone and sits on top of it with the baby on her lap. The pouring rain pelts her skin, causing goosebumps to form and her teeth to chatter as she continues to unwrap a makeshift tablecloth from the baby's naked body.

Subjected to her life's harsh conditions, the baby is smaller than the typical newborn, and its limbs appear underdeveloped. Vascular veins streak its skin, resembling spun spider webs, draping its premature torso toward its unclipped belly-button cord.

Sounds of a crying baby echo through the alleyway. Thinking they are coming from her small boy, she embraces the child tighter to comfort it. "All will be good; I will protect you from their grasp," she says.

Laughter sounds from the corner of the brick walls, and her head jerks up to look. A flash of lightning exposes the creature's long arms stretching towards them. Its spindly fingers release a snap, causing her to suffer sudden paralysis.

Her speech freezes in her mouth, and she gasps for air as the tiny corpse tumbles from her useless arms to her lap. With another snap of the skeleton's thin fingers, her head jerks up, and her mouth gapes open. Unable to swallow, she chokes as her throat fills with water from the heavy rain trickling past her tongue. The arms retract into the darkness, and light footsteps approach as she remains helplessly kneeling, trapped in the jarring position.

Thunder resounds, and a peculiarly bright lightning strike showcases Daniel's body emerging from the corner. He proudly walks with a swagger, his chest puffed to the dark sky. He stands over the woman and, ignoring her, carefully leans forward to pick the child up from her lap. As the severed umbilical cord trails behind it, he chuckles. "If you are to be great, you must look the part," he says. He bares his teeth into a smile, revealing their sharpened pearly edges.

Her lungs, struggling not to drown, cough up water as they gurgle three words before hacking retakes her speech. "Don't touch him!"

His lips curl at the sound of her dismay. Placing the unnaturally small body in his left hand, he grabs hold of the cord's rotting skin and, bite by bite, devours it. As the stringy flesh vanishes from sight, his gnawing teeth reach the baby's belly button, and, with one last bite, he pulls away to behold the child. "With that done, we are one. Given that I have devoured your flesh, you will come to be a vessel for our success," he says as he glances at the shadow in the corner.

"Come, come, come," calls a voice from the darkness.

Swiftly, holding the fetid corpse, he follows the beckoning call, much the same as being pulled into a magnetic orbit, and they disappear as one into the alley's pitch-black shadows.

Thunder strikes in the sky with the intensity of fighting lions' roars, and the raucous clamor suddenly snaps her out of her water-logged imprisonment. Drenched, her upper body keels over to catch her breath.

Without warning, her ears fill with the sound of a child's laughter. Her eyes dart in every direction, searching for the origin of the sound. Finally, they come to rest on a peculiar presence emerging from the murky corner. It is an adolescent child!

As the figure exits the dark, a sliver of moonlight hits its face, revealing a small boy dressed in a dark-green velvet suit, matching knickers, polished black dress shoes, and a white ruffled shirt, with his dark-brown hair perfectly quaffed. His eyes are black, with a slight dusting of a light honey glaze, and his skin resembles porcelain. The entirety of his presentation is picture-perfect. It is as if he stepped out of Lambton's "Little Boy in Red" with the additions of green velvet, a cane, and a tiny top hat matching that of his father. The mature way of dressing resembles a miniature adult man, and the way he carries himself reflects twenty years into his senior.

Her motherly instincts kick in, and she knows he is her baby, although he strikes her as different. Even though the circumstance is extremely odd, her seemingly alive and healthy son brings tears of joy to her eyes. She doesn't care whether he is young or old, just that he is hers.

Overjoyed, she wants to confirm her suspicion and stammers to speak. "E-Edgar?" she asks.

The child responds to the name with a devious smirk and a tip of the brim of his hat with his privileged hand. As he steps closer to her, the rain stops, and the alley's darkness somewhat dissipates, revealing a petite figure standing behind him.

Her gaze shifts past Edgar to a small girl, who is identical and quietly follows in his wake. Upon the girl's petite frame is a matching green velvet dress, with a frilly bonnet covering her darkened curls, and her rosy cheeks perfectly accent her long eyelashes. The two children's eyes match in color, and they resemble mannequins in a tailor-shop window showcasing the most expensive children's clothing designs.

Her eyes widen as her cautious pupils dart back and forth between the two children standing side-by-side. It's as though she has seen a ghost.

The facial expression of the young boy exhibits callousness as he comes closer. He leers at her with disgust for her appearance. "You look unwell, mother," he says. The meek girl follows sheepishly behind him.

Still kneeling on the ground and dumbfounded, the woman stares in awe at the two children.

Edgar sneers at her and chuckles. "My father is gone, if that is what you are wondering," he says as he glances back at the corner.

The little girl giggles.

Turning towards his mother, Edgar smirks. "Now, mother, do not forget to greet Louise," he says, gesturing toward the female child.

As she attempts to grasp the situation, she surveys the little girl, then her son. "But I only had one," she says.

He lifts his hand to silence her. "You are, without a doubt, quite funny, mother. Do you not remember your fall? As the two of us were ushering you to the store, you caught your toe on a cobblestone and tumbled to the ground. We have been waiting for you to awaken. You have always had two children—twins," he says.

His elbow bends, and he offers her his arm. "Come along, mother; we mustn't linger in places like this." He dramatically shudders as he scans the garbage on the ground. "I fear you will not be around much longer, so it's best we get going," he says.

She is stunned by his harsh words. "What do you mean? I have suffered no injury."

Edgar glances at his sister and chuckles as if telling an inside joke as he extends his elbow closer. "Let us not dally; we must go straight away," he says.

Her body doesn't move.

"Now!" he commands.

She promptly nods and glances back to the corner where the children first appeared. Thinking she's caught sight of the whites of Daniel's eyes, her hand lunges to grasp Edgar's extended arm, and a tickle forms in her throat upon touching it. She lifts her opposite hand to cover her cough, and as she retracts it from her mouth, she notes a spattering of blood. She attributes it to the stressful circumstances, brushes herself off, and stands.

"Very good. Now, let us walk," Edgar says with a smirk. With a last look at the corner, he ushers her out of the dismal alley while glancing over his shoulder to ensure his sister follows silently behind.

As they make their way through the oddly abandoned streets, Edgar takes a moment to impart to his mother the critical information he was told by the shadowy figure to relay. "Things may be taxing, mother, especially since you have no husband and two children to care for. But as you know, Louise doesn't require much food, so she shouldn't weigh much on our finances." He glances at her to make sure she is listening. "Before father left us, he bequeathed me several rules we must follow," he says.

Hearing him refer to Daniel makes her cringe and irks her soul. "Oh, is that so?" she asks. Before she allows him to continue, she becomes defensive. "It is my house, not his, so I set the rules for my children, not him," she says.

He giggles at her remark. "He predicted you may say that. To assure you take care of us correctly this time, he will send his mother to check on us after we're tucked in each night. He said not to be frightened, because she means well. The only courtesy we must offer is leaving her a piece of cake outside our doors every evening at bedtime."

As his mother listens, she clears her throat to clarify. "Cake?" she asks.

"Yes, any type. She is not particular," he says.

"What happens if we refuse?" she asks.

He stares off into the distance and smirks. He shrugs, and he pauses. At once, his expression shifts, losing every sign of emotion as his mind drifts into a momentary daydream. Turning towards his mother, he gives her a devilish grin. "She will just find something else to eat," he says.

Edgar's similarity to his father is unsettling, and the revelation causes her to gasp. The little girl giggles at the mother's nervousness.

"You will find it best to leave the cake as required," Edgar says.

His mother clears her throat and silently nods.

They pass the last streetlamp lighting their way and turn down a walkway leading to a rundown brick brownstone. The small boy lowers his arm to release his mother's grasp and points to the stairs. "Ladies first," he says.

Wanting to go to bed, hoping to wake the following day free from the horrible nightmare, she takes a quick step forward, and her shaking hands anxiously grab the stair's iron railing for stability. Arduously, she makes her way to the door. A frigid breeze rolls through the street and creates icicles on her damp skin while she pats her dress to find her keys. Before she can pull them from her pocket, Edgar shouts from the bottom step, "It is unlocked."

With everything in her, she refrains from looking back at him. Wanting to escape the treacherous chill, her hand darts to the silver handle of the door, and it quickly turns underneath her fingers. Her eyes widen, and her jaw clenches as she stands frozen in fear.

Edgar notices her lack of movement and gets annoyed that she is not going inside. "They are just trying to help, and nothing more," he says.

She can feel the warmth of a burning fire inside the home teasing her frost-bitten skin, and her desire takes over.

As she makes her way through the entrance, the children stay at the base of the steps. Seeing that she is too far away to hear them, they turn to one another for a discussion.

Like a child playing a game of telephone, Edgar's hands cup around his mouth to whisper in Louise's ear. "Shall we remind her of the cake?" he asks.

The little girl quietly giggles to herself and shrugs.

Edgar can tell what she is thinking, and redirects the conversation before she can speak. "You are right, Louise; she is a liability to the plan. I'm not sure how we arrived from her lineage. She is quite the catastrophe," he says.

She smiles at the darkness inside the open door.

One by one, a set of unrecognizable fingers wrap around the right side of the door frame. Each of the nails is jagged and thick in texture, and the fingers' severely wrinkled skin, discolored with gray and brown splotches, drapes over the obscenely long bones. As they coil around the frame, the tips of the nails lightly tap the wood.

The children smile at one another.

The creature's head finally emerges from the darkness to peek around its coiled hands, revealing only the upper half of its face. Long white hair, mounded on its head in a frizzy updo secured with a bone hairpin, matches its eyebrows, which are so light that they appear nonexistent. The skin masking its decrepit face is a whitish-gray tone. Unlike what one may expect, considering the look of the creature's shriveled hands, the skin's tautness remains preserved, stressing the protrusion of the lidless black pupils of its non-blinking eyes.

Its presence causes the small boy's eyes to twinkle as if seeing a long-lost friend. "Grandmother," he says.

The sound of his recognition causes the upper bridge of the creature's nose to scrunch, signifying the formation of a smile.

As the two share a moment eyeing one another, loud footsteps echo towards the front door, and the creature disappears, replaced by their mother's face and her snapping fingers as she beckons their attention through the door's opening.

Edgar apathetically stares at her, frustrated by her behavior.

Promptly, her hand covers her mouth to shield a cough. She feels she is losing control of her child and shifts her demeanor to demand order. "Edgar, come inside before you contract a case of consumption," she says, pointing her bloody palm towards him.

"Yes, mother," he replies. As she retreats inside, he peers back at his sister. "You're right. We must get rid of her. She will die regardless, so she should thank us for ending her misery." He reaches for his sister's hand and leans toward her to tell her a secret. "I would much prefer Grandmother as my mother."

Louise squeezes his hand and silently nods, smiling.

They race each other up the steps, and once inside, the door slams behind them.

Chapter 2

CAKE

The door slamming shut creates an echo through the home's narrow hallway, and the children laugh.

The sounds of their mother's storming feet race from the kitchen towards them. Stopping near the entry, she points to the staircase. "You two need to be off to bed," she says.

Her assertive tone causes their laughter to grow louder as they push past her to head toward the kitchen at the end of the hall. Set back by their behavior, she turns around in disbelief and chases behind them. Their feet leave a trail of muddy water that spreads across the home's dark worn wood flooring with her bustling steps.

As the children enter the kitchen, they scan the perimeter for a slice of cake. The rectangular room is relatively small. A wooden butcher block with various deep scratches sits in the middle of the space, and upper and lower rows of light-colored unfinished oak cabinets line the wall behind it. Tucked amongst the cabinets is a rundown bread oven with a layer of peeling white paint and a makeshift sink made of tin stands on four metal legs next to it.

Committed to their quest, the children swiftly split up as if playing a scavenger hunt game, each searching high and low for the baked prize. They run in opposite directions around the chopping block, rummaging through every cabinet they can reach.

As they try to see who can find a piece of the dessert the fastest, Edgar's mother barrels into the room. She is livid over the children's disobedience, and her face is a shade of red. The sight of the tiny humans creating a mess fuel her rage, and she stomps her feet for them to stop. Her sudden movements cause her lungs to hack, and, covering her mouth, she loudly coughs. "Stop this at once!" she says as she wipes the blood from her palm onto the skirt of her damp dress.

Both ignore her as they crawl around in the lower cabinets.

Not being able to see what they are doing frustrates her, and the sound of clinking pots agitates her nerves. She screams at the top of her lungs. "In God's name, what are you ravenous children doing in there?" she asks. Trying to get their attention, she frantically claps her hands. "Tell me this instant."

Louise, unaffected by the sound, continues rummaging, but, sensitive to loud noises, Edgar covers his ears as he retreats backward from the cabinet. He calmly swivels his feet to turn towards her with a condescending smile. "Are you trying to deafen me, mother?" he asks.

She continues, ignoring his question. "Why are you making a mess of my kitchen when you know this behavior is unacceptable?"

Standing tall, Edgar puffs his chest and brushes the knees of his velvet knickers, smoothing the grain of the fabric in the same direction. "It is rather simple. Did you not listen to a single word I told you on our stroll home?"

Her lips purse together, and her irritation becomes unquestionable. "Disrespectful little—" she says before Edgar interrupts her.

"I caution you to stop before you say something you may regret. I clearly explained that father instructed us we must have cake to feed the old woman sent to check on us each night."

His combination of small stature and ridiculous verbiage makes her cackle. As she prepares to confront him, she shifts the tone of her voice to one of sarcasm. "Oh, yes, that is right. Your father gave us rules to follow," she says, using her hands to mime the words.

The child rolls his eyes. She rushes across the kitchen and grabs hold of his arm. "Enough of this ridiculous escapade. You are going to bed now!" she says. Her head shifts to the back of Louise's dress sticking out from a cabinet. "That goes for you, too!"

The sound of rummaging promptly stops, and Louise crawls out from the pan-filled cubby. Quietly shutting the door, she stands and glances at the floor.

The mother snaps her fingers to get her attention. "Don't dilly-dally, child; move along."

She tightens her grip around the boy's arm, and he flinches. "Ow, you are hurting me. You are nothing more than a hedge-creeping ratbag," he says.

Angered by his disrespect, she ignores his insults and continues to drag him to the staircase, with his sister following closely behind.

She prepares for the lack of lighting they will encounter by grabbing a burning candle from a wall sconce mounted near the entry.

Each worn wooden tread creaks underneath their feet as they make their way up the stairs. Upon reaching the top, a narrow hallway decorated with floral-print wallpaper greets them. Though once pristine, it is now marred with blotchy brown water stains.

There are two doors at opposite ends of the hall. Behind one is the mother's sleeping quarters, and the other conceals the children's room.

She leads them to the end of the corridor and opens their door. Blindly reaching into the dark room, she lights a candle mounted to the wall, then swiftly ushers them inside.

As the children enter, they note that the room only holds a single child's crib. "This is absurd. There is nowhere for us to sleep," Edgar says as he marches around the room, assessing the paltry accommodations.

"Don't be ungrateful. I will go fetch something that will do," his mother says while exiting to gather spare blankets, sheets, and pillows from her room. As she returns with an armful of bedding, she notices the kids' discontentment and, tired of dealing with it, she tosses the items to the middle of the floor.

Angered, Edgar opens his mouth to spew his thankless opinion. Unwilling to listen, she swiftly leaves the room and slams the door. "Goodnight! Sleep tight!" she says as she twists the lock.

Their accommodations disgust Edgar, but he is relieved to be locked in a room devoid of her company. He turns toward his sister and grins. "Well, at least we have each other," he says. Louise nods. "What do you say we make the best of the situation? I believe making a fort from this pile of rags would be utterly brilliant," he says as he sorts the bedding, evaluating his options.

His sister follows along and snatches up a pillow.

Shifting his focus to the crib, Edgar rushes to the wooden bed and removes the thin cotton pad from the bottom. "This will have to do. We cannot allow our lineage to suffer contact with a cold, filthy floor," he says, shivering and thinking how his back might suffer as he sets the small mattress on the ground next to the crib. Using the wooden rails, he strategically hangs white sheets over the sides and drapes them to the floor, creating a makeshift tent. Playing along with her brother's creativity, Louise passes him more bedding to assist in setting up the fort.

After laying the last pillow beneath the shelter, they step back. Admiring the finished product, Edgar reaches over, lightly pats Louise's back, and nods with a sense of accomplishment. She responds with a smile.

At once, he remembers the rules Daniel instructed them to follow. Now locked in the room and unable to scavenge for cake, he becomes nervous for their safety. He sets his top hat on the floor in the corner and paces from wall to wall, formulating a plan. "What are we to do? We have no cake for Grandmother," he says as he turns around to face his sister.

Rather than worried, Louise is calm. Her body silently leans forward, and she pulls something from the lace sock concealed beneath her ankle-length dress. To his surprise, a small piece of cake rests in her hand, and she smirks pridefully.

Edgar's eyes light up with excitement as he sprints across the room to her. "Where did you get that from?" he asks. He takes a step back while surveying the cake in her palm. Concerned that his tone may have come across as jealous of her beating him to the solution; he changes his approach. "Never mind, dear sister. The only thing that matters is that we will be safe."

Her lips smirk as her hand extends the small, stale piece of pound cake toward him. Knowing they are running out of time, he carefully collects the offering from her hand and, carrying it with great care, makes his way towards the door. "Father said we must set it outside," he says. His hand grasps the knob and gives a forceful turn, but the door refuses to open. Suddenly, he remembers his mother locked it upon her exit. "Damn it!" he shouts.

The sound of the mother retiring to her room and closing her door triggers an idea. Crouching, he presses the bread-like texture between his palms to flatten it. "That should be adequate," he says. Carefully placing it on the floor, he scoots it through the gap under the door to the other side.

Standing, he turns to address his sister. "That will have to do. I am confident grandmother will understand." Her body language shows her agreement.

Edgar makes his way to their fort made of linens and, in a gentleman-like manner, holds one of the sheet flaps up, allowing his sister to enter. "Ladies first," he says. She skips inside with a huge grin and sits on the mat. After taking one last scan of the room to assure they are safe, he enters behind her. Gently letting the makeshift door fall back to the floor brings a sense of relief.

He helps tuck her in, then lays next to her on the mat and pulls the covers over his body. He rolls to his side and gazes at the single candle's flicker illuminating the thin walls. "I know you are shy and should never feel compelled to speak, regardless of who may pressure you. Just remember, as your twin, I know your thoughts, and can always answer for you," he says as he turns to face her.

She is both relieved and comforted by his reassurance. Letting out a yawn, she smiles.

He yawns with her, and as he rolls over, he smirks. "Goodnight," he says.

Their eyes gradually close. As they drift to sleep, the candle flame slightly sizzles as it goes out, leaving the children in complete darkness.

A cupboard door in the kitchen releases a creak as it opens. The exertion used to slam the door shut causes the hinged wood to bounce a few times, and the noise of the resulting crash echoes through the hallway.

Edgar's eyes spring open. His body, paralyzed by uncertainty about what is forthcoming, stares at the sheet ceiling above his head. "She is here," he says as he taps his sister lying beside him.

As her groggy eyes open, she glances at her brother to see what's wrong and hears lumbering footsteps making their way up the staircase to the hallway.

Remaining still, Edgar raises his pointer finger to his lips, signaling for her to be quiet, and she responds with a single nod of compliance. His hands carefully grab the blanket covering them, and, making no jarring movements, he pulls it over their heads to hide.

The footsteps grow louder, then abruptly stop outside the door to their room.

With their eyes tightly closed, they listen as the creature crouches. Its nails scrape against the floor like scampering mice as it collects the cake between its fingertips.

Then, everything falls silent.

Thinking that they have pleased her, they lower the cover from their eyes as the gut-wrenching sound of the door opening meets their ears. The handle rapidly fidgets, and the two hide behind the blanket, terrified they are no longer safe.

Using its fingernail, the creature picks the door lock through the skeleton-shaped keyhole. It pushes the heavy wooden entry open with a single flick of a nail, and the lack of momentum causes the hinges to produce an eerie groan as it gradually creeps open. Each barefooted step sounds sticky as the figure moves closer to the children's hiding spot.

The entity's trickster behavior tests their bravery. They pull the covers higher over their faces and clasp each other's hands as they hear the sheet wall near their feet rub against the skin of the creature's dry fingers.

Lifting the white fabric, the being elongates its neck and peers inside. Not seeing the children, it claims the fort as its lair to devour its prize. With the cake in hand, it lowers its naked, shriveled body to the floor and crawls inside with its breasts and belly dragging against the worn wooden planks.

The children hold their breath to stay silent.

Its bony kneecaps rub the floor as it makes its way underneath the tent's most significant peak. As it repositions itself in a crouch directly under the tent's center, a giant crooked smile takes over its face, exposing its peculiarly shaped teeth. Each tooth is long, thin, and resembles a sharpened porcelain pencil. There are no gaps between them as they perch, perfectly placed for devouring whatever crosses their path.

The piece of cake excites the creature, and the smell of vanilla makes its nostrils flare. Shifting its body, it unknowingly perches directly over the top of the children's hiding spot while devouring the small offering.

Crumbs rain down on the blanket that shields their faces. Each tiny crumble hitting their covering makes tinkling noises, like small rain droplets falling against a tin shack's roof. They try not to squirm as each bit surprises them with a light tap.

At their wit's end and still holding their breath, the children hear a shuffling noise from the mother's room at the other end of the hall. Mid-bite, the monstrous being arches its back, pushing it against the cloth ceiling as it releases a loud roaring shriek, and as its head lowers back in the children's direction, it shoves the last nibble of the smashed cake into its mouth with a devilish grin. Chewing, it silently waits.

The door down the hall slams against the wall, and there's the sound of footsteps trekking through the narrow corridor towards the ravenous guest.

Edgar lies silently, grinning underneath the covers, as the creature hovers above. The demonic being crouches over the children in a frozen state, one foot on either side of the mattress, mimicking a stone gargoyle as it waits for her arrival. The echo of the approaching footsteps becomes louder, and it sniffs the air to inhale the scent of her flesh.

Each sound helps paint a picture of what is to come, and the anticipation excites the children. Stiffening their bodies, they try not to squirm, channeling their soundless cheers through their clenched smiles.

The handle to the bedroom door aggressively turns, the wooden entrance flies open, and their mother angrily stands in the opening, tapping her foot. Her body is adorned in a flowing white nightgown, and her long, loosely braided hair cascades past her right shoulder. Clutching a candle in her left hand, she raises the flickering light, hoping to glimpse the child causing the commotion. As she leans forward to get a better peep, melted beads of cream-colored wax drip to the floor, and the tilted candle's light illuminates the bottom half of her livid face. "I thought I told you to go to sleep!"

Her head scans to decipher the details of the mess they have created, and her eyes notice a trail of crumbs by her feet. Bending to the floor, she picks up one of the tiny bits and, holding it between her two fingers, rubs them together to feel the texture.

Everyone in the confines of the tent remains silent.

Still in a contorted squat, the creature's grin elongates, revealing its teeth. Its nostrils flare as it shifts to face the flimsy wall of sheets. It quietly leans forward as it rests on the callused balls of its splotchy feet, observing the mother's tantrum through a crack in the overlapping cloth. With a single nail, it hooks the shelter's finished edge and exposes the left half of its face as it peeks around the corner.

The mother, confirming the crumb's texture to be cake, glares at the tiny morsel between her fingers. "You stole food from the kitchen? All you do is take!" She waits a moment to receive a response, her breathing growing heavy. Not hearing an apology from her children adds to her fury, and, sticking the candle out in front of her, she curses the kids' father while moving toward the sconce on the wall to re-light it.

As her back turns, the creature silently creeps from the tent one limb at a time. Leaving its weight on the balls of its feet, it rises leisurely to an upright position as a grin remains plastered across its face. The sound of the wick's newly lit flame crackles, and it straightens up to glare at her as its glossy black pupils mirror the flickering orange flame.

Engulfed by thoughts of the children's menacing behavior, the mother's mind fixates on her hateful irritation towards them. "All I ask is for the respect owed to me!" Her skin basks in the feeling of warmth from the newly lit candle's heat, and she smiles at the punishment she is preparing to unleash on the rambunctious kids for defying her. Her confidence is unwavering, and her ego flourishes as she fills with a sense of control. Tilting her nose into the air to show her disdain, she closes her eyes to gather her rage and turns to face the tent to unleash it.

Her eyes and mouth spring open in unison, but not a single word exits her lips.

Each bounce of the flame flickering behind her, created by the candle held by her trembling hand, unveils the decrepit figure's outline.

The creature stays still as its head tilts to the right with curiosity.

As it straightens its head to face her, she swiftly takes a step back, and the candle she's clutching in her hand extinguishes.

The creature's head readjusts, revealing a better view of its demonically possessed eyes. Saliva builds in its mouth and forms tiny spittle bubbles that pulse between its sharpened teeth with every breath. "Cake?" it asks.

Remembering what Edgar had said, she scrambles to the floor, frantically searching for crumbs to offer the entity.

It lifts its knees, kicking each forward one by one as they lead its body in a march toward her. She continues to search the ground, unaware that it has crossed the room and now hovers over her, waiting for an offering.

A drop of thick saliva hits the back of her neck, and her eyes briefly close. Her hands neurotically brush the darkened wood floor in the dimly lit room, sweeping up any crumb she encounters. She gulps nervously as she attempts to piece three small cake dots together.

The monstrous entity chuckles at her fear, and each laugh releases a lungful of air filled with the stench of rotting flesh.

She timidly stands, thinking she will get out of the terrifying predicament. She cups her perspiring hands together to hide the pitiful offering. "Of course I have your cake," she says. Trying to ease suspicion, her eyes stare directly into its enlarged pupils, and she extends her cupped hands toward it.

Its nostrils let out a puff of air as it attempts to smell the surrounding air to guess the flavor. Unable to catch a whiff of a sweet delectable, it repeats its question with a shifting smile. "Cake?" it asks.

She jiggles the contents inside her cupped palms like one might shake a snow globe.

The thing's hands wiggle at its sides in anticipation. Suddenly, it snatches and holds her clasped hands between its enormous, elongated palms. With its missing eyelids, it cannot squint to get a better view, so instead, it bulges its left eye out of its skull to focus its sight. Even with the added effort, it still cannot see through the woman's skin, and it grits its snarling teeth, forcing the eye to protrude closer. Gaining too much momentum, the left eyeball vigorously pops from its socket and, still attached to a long vein, bounces like a paddleball against the abnormally tight skin on its cheek.

Trying to keep calm, the woman can't help staring at the monstrous creature's empty socket, and the sight causes her to tremble.

As the creature senses her growing terror, it indicates that it is only after the cake by shifting its demeanor. With a light grunt, it slightly nods its head and softens its smile to show its intentions. Analyzing its energy, her nerves calm, and she feels more at ease for a moment.

Knowing their mother doesn't have an offering to give makes the lack of physical tussling and deficiency of hostile sounds confusing, and the children become impatient. They eyeball one another in silence, quietly agreeing on how to proceed, and, both wanting to view the event, inch out from under the covers.

Together, the children sit on the edge of the mat, facing the white sheet wall. The candle's light secured to the wall casts shadows of the mother and monster. The flimsy divider projects the unfolding scene as they enthusiastically watch the shapes of each character performing in the shadow puppet show.

Without removing the colossal smile from its face, the creature draws the mother's hands closer to the level of its eyes, excited over obtaining its second delectable treat. Its lips curl, baring each tooth, and the vein attached to its eyeball coils back inside its skull. A sucking sound echoes throughout the room as the eye pops back into position and spins in a circular motion while observing her hands.

The woman sneers, thinking she has outsmarted the creature. It deeply giggles with building anticipation, acting like a child unwrapping a gift. One-by-one, its icy digits pry open the fingers of her left hand as it salivates, waiting to take a gander at the prize.

Her empty palm confounds the being, and, provoked by the lie, it grabs her by the wrist and shakes the destitute hand, sending the three measly crumbles cascading to the floor.

The woman finds the monster's perplexed expression entertaining, and a wild smirk forms on her lips. "It's invisible," she says. Not thinking it understood her retort, she dramatically shrugs and chuckles.

The children delightedly smile at one other as they behold the shadowy interaction displayed across the sheet's surface.

Provoked by the lack of cake, the creature peers at her mid-shrug, then shoves her empty hand in its mouth.

With one last smile, it gives a severing chomp, releasing her from the clench of its bite.

The action happens so swiftly that she doesn't realize her hand is gone until she hears her bone snapping underneath its grinding teeth. The onset of excruciating pain causes her to scream at the top of her lungs.

Blood sprays the room from the severed artery in her wrist, and Edgar flinches with a grin as crimson splatters the sheet.

A stray finger hangs from the creature's mouth as it chews. Each crunch of bone is louder than the last as it savors the sweet taste.

Weakened from blood loss, the woman attempts to stop the bleeding by using her opposite hand's fingers as a tourniquet around her severed wrist. Terrified and desperate to escape, she falters as she moves toward the door. With every labored step, the storm outside churns more violently, rattling the shutters and forcing the howling wind through the open window. The moment she reaches her escape, its surge gains momentum, and the force slams the door closed in her horrified face.

Not wanting to release her grip around the dissected bone, she turns with the limb in hand, searching for another exit. Her eyes meet the room's only window, which is across the chamber, in the far corner. With a blustering gust, the corner darkens, filled by the entrance of the shadow.

The carnivorous entity finishes its last swallow, then makes an eerily slow descent towards her. Panicked about what it will do next, she points her handheld stubbed arm at it and shouts, "Get back! I'm warning you!"

The wind forms a tunnel-like tornado within the bedroom walls. It rustles and lifts the sheets off the ground.

The siblings silently gaze in awe, holding on to one another and mentally cheering each step the creature takes toward the woman.

Fighting the storm infiltrating through the open window makes every step to the exit harder than the last. It is as if she's moving in slow motion. The added energy she must use to fight the pushing of the wind increases the flow of blood through her veins, expediting the bleeding at the amputation site.

Finally making it to the window's edge fills her with a sense of safety. She protrudes the upper half of her body through the opening to survey the distance from the second story to the ground below.

Loud crashes of thunder sound from above, rattling the window's hinges.

The shakiness of the wooden framing surrounding the frosted glass jars her body, and she flails her limbs to shuffle her weight forward to escape. Not feeling any momentum helping to get her out the window, she turns to see the creature maintaining a hold on her nightgown with a smile. As she kicks her feet to free herself, the rocking motion causes the window frame to shake, and the window crashes down against her ribcage with a cruel thump. Trying to scream for help, she coughs up blood.

The creature's grin lengthens as it yanks her back inside with a violent tug, and her body thuds to the floor. It finds enjoyment in the air being knocked from her lungs, and, lowering itself, it crawls on top of her. Glaring directly into her eyes, it welcomes her terror. As its jaws part, its lips stay curled in the shape of a crooked smile, and with a deep inhalation, it devours her soul.

The children lean forward with excitement as it sucks the life from every inch of her body.

As the last bit of plasma-rich oxygen dissipates from her veins, her face petrifies like a piece of driftwood shaped into the expression of her scream, and her skin shrivels to a mummy-like appearance.

Finished with devouring the woman's inner being, the creature strokes the skin underneath its neck as it gradually regains its elasticity. Using her sternum as a springboard, it pushes off her chest, helping itself to stand. After admiring the deflated corpse, its grin widens as its long fingers grasp a handful of her braid.

The children hold one another tighter as they witness their mother's body being dragged towards the door.

Before the creature reaches the handle, the door creaks and automatically opens. The weight of the carcass causes the being's back to hunch as it tugs it along behind its lumbering steps. As it makes its way into the hall, it snaps its spindly fingers, and the door slams shut behind it.

Huddled on the mat, the children reflect on what they've just witnessed. Their eyes widen, and they eye one another in unison with matching smirks.

Edgar scans the trail of bodily fluids smearing the floor and stippling the sheets. He stands, laughing, and paces the room, pretending to be their mother. "Someone made a mess!" he says.

His sister silently giggles at his act and claps. He bows at the applause and gallops back to the small mattress. "Well, dear sister, we had better get some rest before the sun rises. I have a hunch our lives will change for the better starting tomorrow. Most certainly, our accommodations will improve, thank God," he says.

She happily scoots herself to her side of the tiny sleeping quarters and pats the space next to her with her right hand. As he snuggles beside her, Edgar releases a yawn and lays his head on the pillow next to her. The room's temperature drops from the frigid air entering the open window. He reaches for the blanket at their feet, and as he pulls it over them, he glances at the matching velvet outfits on their bodies. "Thank God our clothing remained pristine." He gasps at the horrid thought. "We always must put our best foot forward, and that starts with our attire," he says as he releases another yawn.

Tired, Louise yawns along with him and closes her eyes.

The shadow in the room's corner exudes a comforting warmth. "Sleep tight, little ones, sleep tight," it whispers.

They smile as they drift to sleep, knowing they will have a new beginning in the morning.

The notion brings them the utmost joy.

Chapter 3
FRESH START

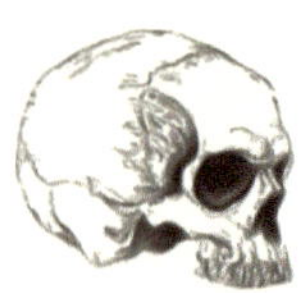

The children lie asleep upstairs as the sun rises in the sky. Even though the light does not shine through the window, an enormous shadow remains cast over their still bodies, restoring their energy and preparing them for what the day may bring. It is so comforting that not even a squawking bird can wake them from their slumber. As they dream sweet dreams of riches, the prediction of a new beginning manifests outside.

A grand carriage that does not fit in with the surroundings pulls up in front of the rundown brownstone. The cabin's exterior is a deep navy blue, with gold and white details outlining each door. The rare sight instantly attracts the attention of the impoverished residents, who immediately surround the well-to-do transportation to beg for money.

A seasoned driver named Frederick sits at the helm, wearing an extravagant patterned navy outfit to complement the carriage's exterior. A single peacock's feather majestically plumes from the side of his matching beaver-felt top hat, adding a bit of panache to his formal attire.

Hopping from the front seat with a spring in his step, he opens the passenger-side door closest to the townhome's entrance. The impoverished townspeople, shoeless and wearing tattered and stained rags for clothing, try to glimpse the cabin's passenger.

Before the door can fully open, a man with emerald-green eyes uses his black cane to push it. "That's quite alright; I shall take it from here, Frederick," he says.

"Yes, sir," Frederick says with a nod while taking a step back and peering down at the grimy cobblestone.

He enters the open air, one leg after the other, and the townspeople gawk at his perfectly matched black outfit with its satin-trimmed edges and buttons made from mother-of-pearl. He is thin and statuesque. Everything, including the stubble on his chiseled chin, is perfectly proportioned.

An older woman from the crowd pretends to faint at the sight, and she fans herself to get his attention. "I prayed for a man such as you to come and rescue me. Thanks be to God. He has listened to my pleas," she says.

Ignoring her flirtatious remark, he directs his attention to the weathered front door. "I suppose that is it?" he asks the driver as his head nudges toward the run-down brick brownstone.

"Afraid so, sir," Frederick says, glancing in the same direction. Noticing the man's discomfort, he offers assistance. "Shall I accompany you?"

The man takes a deep breath and puts on a brave front. Puffing his chest, he dramatically taps his cane against the uneven ground. "This is my family's debacle and my responsibility, not yours," he says as he ushers Frederick to stay with his raised hand. The driver nods and, grabbing the dark bay horse's reins, hops in the driver's seat to wait at his post.

As the man makes his way to the front door, he attempts to hold his breath to mask the stench of warm piss and shoos off beggars trying to touch him with his silver-encrusted walking stick. His feet gallop up the steps, and his body nervously stands in front of the chipped wooden door. Taking a momentary pause, he glances back at the resting driver for a hint about what he should do.

Frederick dramatically mimes the word "Knock" with his lips and forms his right hand into a ball to give an example.

"Oh, yes," the man says. Not wanting to touch the door, he lifts his cane and gives the entry a few whacks.

No one answers. He raises his walking stick again and hits the door harder.

The sound echoes through the home, causing Edgar's eyes to open. Thinking the grandmother might have returned, he shakes his sister to wake her and springs to his feet. Streams of light pour through the room's shutters, and he jumps over the blood smears as though playing a game of hopscotch as he races to peek outside. His sister sits up with a giant yawn and stretches her arms.

As he peers through the wooden slats, Edgar spots the ornately uncharacteristic transportation, and his eyes light up. Filled with excitement, he shouts to his sister. "Louise! I think someone has arrived to save us!" She gleefully hops to her feet.

While looking out the window, he makes eye contact with the well-dressed fellow knocking on the door and dramatically waves to welcome the visitor.

The man below stares up at the second-story window and yells, "Edgar, is that you?"

"Yes, I shall be right there!" he shouts back, nodding. Running across the room, he fetches his cane and securely places his matching top hat on his head. He makes his way to his sister with an aristocratic walk. Once beside her, he holds out his arm for her to take. She straightens her bonnet and grins from ear to ear as she copies his cocky demeanor with her nose in the air.

Together, they descend the rickety stairs towards the front door.

The man waits impatiently on the front stoop, tapping his foot, wondering what is taking so long. Frustrated, he throws his hands in the air and heads down the steps toward the carriage. The loud, ear-piercing screech of the door opening stops him dead in his tracks, and he turns around. He glances over the top of the children's heads to introduce himself, expecting to address an adult.

They lock eyes and burst into laughter.

Edgar taps his cane against the ground to get the man's attention and clears his throat. "Down here, my good sir," he says.

Their shorter appearances startle the man. Embarrassed by his surprised reaction, he tries to mask his mistake but stumbles over his words. "Oh, my apologies. You must be Edgar... You bear a profound resemblance to your father. I was expecting to speak with whoever oversees you. Please fetch them for me," he says, waving his cane at them.

The small boy stands taller. "There is no caretaker. Louise and I are in charge of ourselves," he says.

The man laughs at the remark and observes the child's angry face. Clearing his throat to stop himself from continuing, he plays along. "Oh... I see," he says, analyzing the young boy's appearance. "I was under the assumption you would be younger."

"Oh? That's peculiar," Edgar says as he glares into his eyes.

The man squints at the child. "Yes, indeed," he says. "I also was under the impression there was only one of you," he says as he extends his cane beside him.

Edgar reaches for the tip of the pointing stick and forces it to lower. "That is correct. There are two of us." He knows if their charade has any hope of success, he will need to persuade the man to listen. He inches his toe a small step closer, and his uncle mimics his action, taking a step back.

Reading his submissive body language, Edgar can tell his tactic is working. "You know, dear sir... With your lack of accurate information about us, I am concerned that you had no acquaintance with my father. If that is the case, I would hate to assume that you are strictly here to prey on two motherless children," he says.

He lowers his voice and scans the crowd of beggars gathering around the ornate carriage. "I shudder to think of having to scream that a predatory stranger is trying to kidnap us under fraudulent circumstances. Considering your fashion sense, that would be a pity."

The passive threat makes the man's face perspire. As his forehead becomes clammy underneath the band of his hat, he gulps and wedges his pointer finger under his collar to loosen it. "I assure you, that is not the case. Your father never mentioned you until after he fled the estate...

Regardless, I am here and uncertain why I am discussing this with you. We must stay on course and not let the past distract us from the task."

Nervously clearing his throat, he stands taller to regain his authority and switches the topic. "Are you certain your mother is not available?"

He steps inside the door, but Edgar calmly reaches out to block his movement. "She is dead, sir," he says. Edgar watches the man turn to ask his sister the same question, and she takes a breath to speak. He places a hand on her shoulder and turns to their guest. "She also confirms she is dead. She is fearfully shy and prefers not to speak, so I speak for her," he says, dramatically shielding her with his arms.

Worried his reputation may become tainted by the child's accusations, the man pauses and scrutinizes Edgar with confusion. "I could turn around now and leave you here in this filth if you prefer," he says.

The comment causes Edgar to think of living in less than pristine conditions another day, and the betrayal creates a shudder that rolls down his spine.

Each hair on his arm stands up as the presence lurks in the shadowed hallway behind him. Its deep voice presents a warm whisper as it enters his eardrum. "Ask him his name, name, name," it says. A warm breath caresses the back of Edgar's neck, making him giggle.

Still staring, the man finds his unprovoked laughter unusual.

The small boy clears his throat and smiles. "If I am to let you into this home, I must inquire about the identity of our guest," he says.

The man's complacency regarding social etiquette embarrasses him as he digests the child's words. He blames the introductory oversight on the distraction caused by their accusations that he is a stranger. His gloved hand shoots forward to shake the small boy's and make an introduction. " Ah, yes, my apologies, young chap, for forgetting my introduction. How rude of me. I am David, your uncle—your father's brother," he says.

Sensing the man to be genuine, Edgar accepts his offer to start over and shakes his hand.

Mid-handshake, the sound of the poor townspeople heckling his driver for monetary means makes David impatient. Retracting his hand, he tries again to enter. "Now that I am no longer a stranger, may I come in?" he asks.

Holding the power position, Edgar pauses and lifts his tiny fingers to stroke his chin. As he ponders, he listens for the shadow to guide him from the hallway. "Let him in, let him in, let him in," it beckons.

The familiar voice immediately brings a sneer to Edgar's face. He moves aside and extends his hand towards the hallway, inviting the man to enter.

David's eyes dart around to ensure none of the peasants follow him, and then his feet sprint inside.

As he races halfway down the hall, the children turn to watch him. While they are all facing away from the entrance, the door slams shut.

The harsh noise causes David to jump and spin around to face the children. He places his hand on his chest. "In God's name, you can't scare a man like that. Give warning before making such a heinous noise."

Both children laugh at his nervousness.

Masking his embarrassment, David paces across the limited square footage of the bottom floor to assess the children's care. The drawn window curtains do not allow a single ray of natural light to enter the confined space. "Bloody Hell, it's dark. Don't you have lamps in here?" he asks as he darts around the room, pulling back the drapes to allow sunlight to penetrate the dingy home.

The children shrug in unison as they watch him rant. The extensive buildup of dust on the red velvet curtains disgusts him, and he tries to wipe his grime-ridden gloves on the water-stained floral wallpaper next to the window. He refrains from touching anything else as he uses the light to better survey the surrounding environment. "This place is unkempt," he says as he walks the short distance to the kitchen.

The cabinets remain open from the cake hunt the night before, and mud from the children's shoes and the mother's flowing petticoat paint the wood.

Confused by the chaotic state of the home, David takes his hat off to scratch his head. "How long did you say it has been since your mother's passing?" he asks. As he waits for a response, he places the hat back on.

Without hesitation, the young boy gives a confident answer. "Since the wee morning hours," he says.

David had been sure she had perished weeks before based on the mess in the house, and his jaw clenches as he tries to process the timeline. "I beg your pardon. You were just orphaned this morning?"

Seeing no issues with the recentness of their orphaning, the children nod in unison.

Even though he can't place his finger on the cause of the aching sensation stemming from his gut, something doesn't feel right to David about the situation. His eyes dart to the staircase. "Fascinating," he says. His curiosity builds concerning the state of the second floor, and he wishes to explore the home further. Before he says another word, he darts towards the staircase.

Edgar gawps at the uncle in disbelief, and as soon as the reality of the situation sets in, he chases after him. "Wait! Don't go up there," he shouts.

The child's abnormally frantic tone causes David to stop halfway up the stairs. "Why not?" he asks.

Edgar stands at the bottom step, scrambling for an excuse to keep David from ascending the staircase, and, running out of options, he cries. A single tear rolls down his cheek, followed by a sniffle to make his act more believable. He glances up to make sure he is buying it.

Watching the child in pain causes David to pause, and the uncle's sympathetic response makes Edgar ramp up more with the hysterics. At the height of his performance, his sister's hand raises behind his back, and she whacks him to get him to tone down the theatrics.

Clearing his throat to mask his frustration with her, he bellows, "Her body is still up there! We are only children; we didn't know what to do when we found her." His tiny hands wipe the fake tears from his eyes as he whimpers.

Witnessing the children's unsanitary environment allows David to understand their emotional responses. He takes a glance upstairs, and the child's waterworks stop.

"She's in her room," Edgar says.

The thought of seeing a dead body causes David's throat to tighten, and he loudly swallows a gulp of air. "Up there?" he asks.

The children nod with sorrowful faces.

"Considering my flesh and blood got you into this mess, it is my duty to get you out." He waves a hand to call the kids to join him. "There is no need to be frightened. I'm certain everything is not as bad as it seems. Now come and show me where she is."

With a complete shift in personality, the children forget to act sad and skip up the steps to lead the way.

Concerned over what he may encounter, David quietly follows behind them.

As they reach the hall, Edgar tells the story of what has happened. "First, let me show you to our room," he says while making his way down the narrow corridor. "Prepare yourself. It may be messy," he says, reaching for the doorknob.

The grown man eyes the small girl for a second opinion, and she smiles in agreement with a big nod.

Turning the handle, Edgar glances over his shoulder as he pushes the door open with a tap of his cane. "You will see that she was not a pleasant woman." With his uncle standing beside him, he uses the end of the stick to point to each reference as he attempts to explain the gruesome scene.

David quickly steps into the room to investigate, and his face immediately turns stark white over the sheer volume of blood and gore spread throughout the space. His voice trembles. "What... what happened?" he asks.

Edgar proudly points to the sizable scarlet smear on the floor and smiles as he fabricates his story. "Our childhood hasn't been easy, especially with her drinking problem. The only saving grace we had with avoiding her beatings was the fact of her body being engulfed by her illness," he says.

David reluctantly inquires further, trying to find the reason for bodily fluid liberally coating the room. "She was sick?" he asks. Wanting to appear educated, he continues with his speculation. "With that much blood, it must have been consumption."

Not thinking of that possibility for the storyline, the child throws his hands up to go along with it. "Your intellect surpasses you. Towards the end, she made a terrible mess, hacking up and spewing that red liquid everywhere. It was by far the worst coughing fit I had ever seen," he says.

The uncle, proud of guessing the illness correctly, fills with a sense of accomplishment. Almost like a real detective solving a crime case, he fills in the blanks on the rest of the narrative. Leaning over the top of the boy, he points to the blood-stained sheet used for the fort. "She must have tried to clean herself up there," he says.

The little boy stops himself from smirking and clears his throat. "Sir, I say you are quite good at this." Switching directions with the tip of his cane, he motions towards the open window, which houses an oblong bloodstain that runs over the ledge and down the wall. "We tried to be helpful by opening the window to get the poor woman some air. She poked her head out briefly, but it seemed to add to her suffering."

David solemnly shakes his head. "She was fortunate indeed to have such attentive children and that you attempted to aid her," he says.

The boy's eyes graze the floor, and he releases a massive sigh of feigned sadness. The sister follows suit, copying his actions.

Filled with compassion for what they have gone through, David ignores bringing up the lack of furniture in the room. "I can't even imagine how hard this must be on both of your angelic souls," he says compassionately, reaching toward them to place a hand on each of their shoulders. After a moment of silence, he identifies the elephant in the room. "Where is her body?"

Slowly turning to peer at him with sorrowful eyes, Edgar fights back a forced tear with a shrug. "She became so livid at our attempt to help that she stormed out of our room to the hallway and shut us inside. We did not follow for fear of getting beaten, so we remained here. This morning, we finally gathered enough courage to peek in her room after the sun rose, and that's when we found her," he says.

The shadowed corner of the room releases a grimacing chuckle that only the children can hear.

Edgar lifts his tiny finger and points to the opposite end of the corridor. "Her room is there," he says. Leaving his hand in the air, he stares down the hall.

The uncle takes a deep breath, and his eyes follow the direction of the small boy's finger. "After you, then," he says, his hand motioning for the children to lead the way.

Edgar flings their door closed and, grabbing his sister by the hand, hurries down the narrow passage towards the woman's room.

David witnesses the children's previous somber walk turn into a gallop as if happily playing a game. Confusion over their behavior stuns him, making his feet stagnant.

Noticing the lack of sound of footsteps following them, they turn around in unison to see to assure grandmother had not gotten him.

A pale hue has fallen over the uncle's stupefied expression. Having no concern for how the gory scene may have traumatized the grown man's mind, the small boy waves his fancy walking stick to grab his attention. "Are you coming?" Edgar asks.

At first glance, David believes the stick is flying toward him, and it causes his anxiety-ridden body to flinch. He takes a moment to regain his bearings on his surroundings and realizes the children have already positioned themselves outside the bedroom door. The heels of his boots click against the floor as he races to join them. He glances at his feet to ensure he doesn't stumble and notes how oddly clean the hallway had remained compared to the mess in the children's room. "The state of your room was quite horrific ... Why did her illness not cause the same level of atrocity out here? Wouldn't a brisk stroll down the hall worsen her condition?"

Pausing for a moment, they glance at one another and lift their brows in silent agreement. Then Edgar answers. "We are small children, dear uncle; we have yet to have the proper schooling to determine such matters. I believe that is a question for the local doctor," he says with a shrug.

As David moves closer, he takes a moment to ponder the logic of the child's response and nods, giving it no more thought.

Enthusiasm to see what the monster has done to finish the mother off tempts Edgar's curiosity, and it gets the best of him. Becoming impatient, he slowly opens the door and, taking a quick look at his sister, notices the permanent grin still plastered on her porcelain face. He wants to smile back, but holds it inside to avoid appearing suspicious.

David gets there just as the door cracks open. He hunches over and rests his weight on his cane to catch his breath. Not wanting to see what's inside, he takes his time after the graphic display he just witnessed in the kid's bedroom.

The children's eyes light up as they see the mother's petrified body lying in her bed. Leaving their uncle behind, they rush inside and circle the corpse.

The texture of her skin resembles a rose hung to dry in the grueling sun, and her face is stuck in an expression of horror. Her eyes are peeled wide open to match the monster's bulging-eyed gawp, and her gaping jaws are locked in a scream.

As the small boy joyously surveys the monster's work, he notices her right arm is the only complete limb sticking out of the covers. Worried over having to explain her missing left hand to the uncle, Edgar glances up and, seeing that he remains positioned in the doorway in a state of shock, he lifts the edge of the covers and takes hold of the mangled arm to shove it underneath. Finding its rigid nature too hard to maneuver, he pushes the limb harder, and the petrified appendage's brittleness causes her arm to snap in two. Edgar shoves the broken limb underneath the covers in a panic.

The uncle jumps, knocked from his catatonic state by the loud crack, and his eyes dart toward the children. "What was that?" he asks. His heart races in terror over the thought of what horrifying scenario his eyes may encounter.

Worried they will get caught in their lies, Edgar pulls the sheets up to cover her head. "It was nothing! I was attempting to hide her death stare from your view. Since you are such a kind soul, we could not bear to see you subjected to more grief," he says.

The idea of shielding himself from viewing further atrocities relaxes David's posture, and, taking a deep breath, he straightens his stance. "Well, that is jolly good news," he says. Stepping inside the room, he stands between the two children and gently places a hand on their backs as a sign of condolence.

Both turn to face him.

His legs fidget, and, not wanting to spend another moment in the home, his nose tips in the air to show his disgust. "It reeks of death in here," he says.

Lowering himself to a squatting position, he meets them face to face as he transitions the conversation to business. "We all must promise that from this moment forward, we will never speak of this again," he says. Upon receiving a nod of understanding, he continues. "This is what we shall do. I will purchase this building and lock it tight, and your mother will remain here to rest in peace. If anyone asks, we will respond that the woman is mentally unstable and prefers to be left to her own devices. Considering how arduous it was for me to locate your whereabouts, I find it extremely unlikely that anyone will inquire, but we must have our stories straight, just in case."

The children glance at one another with a smirk, then stare back at him. Louise mimes locking her mouth with an imaginary key and throwing it away over her shoulder.

Edgar clears his throat. "You don't have to worry about her; she is shy and doesn't favor speaking," he says as he motions his cane toward her. "I won't utter a word."

Swiftly, David springs to his feet and brushes himself off. "Very well, then. Let us make haste," he says. Lifting his chest, he walks with a swagger out the door.

The children follow closely in his wake and carefully close the door behind them.

Lightly touching his small palm to the scratched wood, Edgar whispers, "I will not forget you for your service." Spinning around, he grabs his sister's hand, and they run to catch up with his uncle.

The man suddenly stops and turns, almost causing the children to run into him. "We won't be coming back, so don't forget to grab your belongings," he says.

They eye one another, knowing that the clothes on their backs are the only thing they own.

David's eyes glimpse a pile of garbage at the base of the staircase, and before they can respond, he throws his hands up and interjects. "On second thought, if the room you occupied is any sign of your possessions, and I'm certain that is the case, do not bother. Come with me, and I will buy you a fresh wardrobe," he says as he waves his hand, signaling them to follow. They happily tag along, descending the remaining steps with a huge smile.

Everyone scurries out the home's front door, and with a click of the lock, they walk to the carriage without glancing back.

Chapter 4

WHAT COMES AROUND GOES AROUND

As promised, upon their arrival at David's estate, he purchased the horror-filled brownstone and added the home to the list of Manley Trust properties. Daniel's written words confirmed Edgar's lineage, so they changed his name to Manley, making him the only living heir aside from David, and he welcomed the surname substitution. Daniel never mentioned the little girl, though, making it impossible for David to establish her origin.

He tells the children they both have the family name but secretly avoids the matter, with no luck tracing her birth information. Being the prudent man he is with finances, he wishes to protect his assets, and out of concern for upsetting the small boy, he refrains from bringing the matter up in conversation. As far as he's concerned, all is right as a trivet in his eyes. To him, as a man who typically avoids conflict, that's the best he could hope for.

Even though the environment provides for their every want and need, something unsettling remains surrounding their existence. With each passing day, the children grow skittish, and every sound, including the wind's light breeze, makes them restless. They long for their grandmother, and not seeing her since their mother's grueling death leaves a void in their soul. Though they don't know when, they are confident she will return someday, and the happy thought brings them solace.

At the end of each meal, they patiently wait for the house staff and their uncle to be distracted by conversation. The opportunity proves perfect to collect a hoard of offerings, secretly smuggling any form of cake to their rooms when retiring to bed.

For a moment, they had feared that her lack of presence was due to her not knowing their new location, but the thought swiftly subsided after considering the distance and the fact that the journey by foot may take time. After a bit of pondering, they were confident that she would soon find their new lives and once again check on their circumstances. They always followed the rules, convinced of her imminent arrival.

One may question the cramped sleeping accommodations. *Why would two children share a single room in such a grotesquely large estate?* They did usher the children to separate accommodations when they arrived at the manor, but after quite a dramatic display and demands to remain together, the uncle, convinced that they were still mourning the loss of their mother, abided.

Thinking that his generosity may help his nephew acclimate to the new environment, he willingly complied and, per his request, added a second bed to the chamber.

Within a week, the children grew accustomed to their routine.

Throughout the day, they live carefree, playing jump-rope on the pathways and hide-n-seek in the gardens. Every meal spent sitting together in the formal dining room provides an opportunity to add to their growing collection of stale desserts.

In the late evening, when everything becomes quiet as a church mouse, Louise, the smaller of the two, secretly tiptoes into the hall and, with the utmost care, places an offering at every bedroom door. To keep the secret hidden, she retrieves the baked goods before the rooster crows and the house comes to life and reports to Edgar if any nibbles occurred during the night.

One may assume the task to be easy, but with the hallways lined with creaking floorboards, it's quite the ordeal to go unnoticed. She often refrains from eating to limit her body weight to aid her stealth, and her dwindling, waif-like stature helped each step to be more discreet than the last. Edgar solely attributes the uncle's lack of care to her frail presence.

Everything seems to have been going smoothly until one cold and very dreary evening when the weather is highly reminiscent of their mother's death, with crackling lightning and thunder roaring through the starless night. The children know something is afoot, leaving a trace of bitterness in their mouths, similar to the taste of metallic coins.

On precisely the sixth night from the day of their arrival, at three thirty-three in the morning, an overwhelming feeling that something lingers in the hallway wakes them. Tucked away in bed, Edgar peeks out from under his covers, peering at his sister. Her eyes are open and staring directly at him as she lays silently waiting, hoping to get his attention.

Thump, thump, thump, thump echoes from the hall, replicating the sound one might expect from a body being dragged up a staircase. Familiar grunting sounds emanate from the other side of the door, alerting the children that they have encountered this visitor before.

"Did you place the offering out?" Edgar whispers.

Louise silently nods in reply.

Their eyes dart to the door in unison, anticipating its arrival. Edgar's eyes remain fixed on the entrance as he runs through a mental checklist. "Did you leave something in front of our dear uncle's door?" he asks.

She nods.

"Oh, very good; we still need him if we want to preserve this lifestyle, which I rather enjoy," he says.

She nods and continues to do so as he goes through a list of the house servants.

He nears the end of the long list of names, his demeanor shifts, and his jaw clenches to fight his disdain. "Alice?" he asks. His sister's immediate silence causes him to chuckle. "I mean Ms. Tiller."

The name triggers a unique response in Louise, and her eyes dart around the room to avoid the question.

Edgar's lips quiver with a smirk. "Very good. Very good indeed." He rolls his body over to face his sister's opposing bed, taking a moment of pause. His chest lifts above his tailbone, and he props himself on an elbow to show his assertive thoughts. "Someone must teach her a lesson on being respectful to the heir and heiress of this estate," he says. With a brief chuckle, he thinks of their first steps upon the grand home's entry floor and of how she crushed their happiness.

The leisurely footsteps, after starting a distance down the lengthy hallway, get loud with their creeping approach. One by one, the grandmother wets her fingertips with her slug-like tongue and puts out each candle she passes before checking the coordinating room for a piece of cake. After confirming the sleeping individual has abided by her request, she leans forward, and her bony fingers take hold of the desserts. Snarls add to the crackling sounds of the flickering flames of each lit wick lining the hall.

Knowing the despised maid's room is fast approaching makes the small boy grimace. "I wish I could be in there when it happens," he says. His mind drifts into a dark fantasy, and his voice slightly shifts into an oddly mature texture with gravelly tones. "Just imagine the gawp of her dirt-colored eyes and how scared she will be when she realizes what's coming."

His sister pictures the maid's face, and her lips match his grin, but larger.

Still focused on the ceiling above in anticipation of her demise, Edgar closes his eyes, fighting not to squeal from the eagerness building in his lungs. Even though he has not heard it, he perceives the cracking noise of her bones in his head. As he imagines her limbs snapping like twigs between the creature's long teeth, his smile grows more profound, and his eyes twinkle in the darkness. Cutting him away from the glorious manifestation, he envisions the fear exuding from her hazel eyes as she shrieks in agonizing pain.

Helpless, the discomfort causes her hair to become drenched with sweat as she pleads for assistance. The dull color of her mousy brown hair appears more opulent with the addition of the much-needed moisture, and it contradicts the pastel-yellow nightgown soiled from splattering blood.

The creature bares its teeth, showcasing small pieces of her skin stuck between them.

Even though he was provided the moment to relive justice being served through the vividness of his dream, Edgar's gaze focuses on the maid's facial features and the horror of her wincing. He finds her look of terror like the snooty glance she had given him upon their arrival, and immediately, he relives the moment from the prior week.

As he becomes transported back to the exact moment in his dream, his eyelids flutter.

Both the children are tired from their long day of travel through the countryside to get to their new home. As the bright sunlight through the small window above blinds their groggy eyes, they wake to find a scenic change transpiring outside. With a slight turn of the carriage's wheels, it transports them into an ideal atmosphere of whimsical trees and lush shrubbery.

The inviting sunlight makes everything appear pristine. An eye-catching circular maze of pruned green hedges sits next to the manor's front entry.

David notices his nephew's eyes grow wide with excitement over the circular game of shrubbery. As he watches the child peer out the window, he feels a tinge of guilt. Touching his palm against the boy's shoulder, he tries to compensate for their loss of time by conversing with him. "If you squint hard enough, you can see a glorious fountain that sits in the center," he says as he points over the child's shoulder and out the window.

Both children lean closer to the carriage wall to peer out at the maze formation. "In memory of this day, I shall put a statue of you right on the top," David says.

At first, it excites the young boy to think about a permanent relic erected in his honor, but when he notices his sister's body language shifting, he wipes the happiness from his expression. "What about my dear sister?" he asks.

The question throws off David's contented mood, and he stares back at the boy. As he acknowledges his concern, he softens his demeanor. "I suppose we can find a solution—possibly creating something similar for her in an alternate area of the property," he says as he motions to the seat next to him.

Hearing the news brings excitement back to Edgar as he glances at his sister, and they exchange a smile. Finishing their shared glance, he extends his hand towards his uncle for him to shake. "We have agreed, and we find that resolution suitable," he says.

Unable to hold his excitement, David jumps in his seat. "Cheerio!" he says. "I will get that squared up right away."

As they sit facing each other in silence, the momentum of the carriage wheels abruptly ceases. Each passenger grabs the closest interior feature to stabilize their bodies against the effects of the jarring movement.

"We are home," David says with a smile.

The children look at one another. As their excitement grows, the carriage door clicks open, directing their attention to the fading sunlight entering the cabin.

Frederick pokes his head inside. "Are you ready to see your new home?" he asks. Both children swiftly nod. With a nudge, he motions them to follow him outside as he props the door wide open.

Edgar jumps out and moves into the sunlight. He scans for his sister and notices she is absent. Panicked, he turns to peer back at the carriage's open door.

Still perched inside its confinements, she stays hidden by the shadows. Her shy presence makes him chuckle. "Silly Louise, whatever are you still doing in there?" he says. She playfully shrugs.

He laughs at her as he turns to address the uncle and driver. "My apologies. She is quite shy sometimes," he says.

Trying to mask their confusion, both grown men look at one another to unify their expressions. The boy snaps his fingers to get their attention. "Well, don't just stand there. Someone needs to help her out," he says to the men.

As she shuffles towards the door, the driver follows the young boy's cue and runs to assist her, extending an arm.

She grins at the offer, and, rather than taking his arm, hops down to the ground on her own. Giggling, she runs to stand by her brother's side.

"It's okay, sister; they didn't mean it," Edgar says as he places a hand lightly on her shoulder. Taking a deep breath, he regains his composure and glares at the driver, who hasn't moved. The boy grows impatient with the charade. "We are ready to see our accommodations," he says.

David steps in to smooth over any animosity. "Of course, yes, very well then." He races to wave a hand in front of Fredrick's stunned face, gawping into the darkness of the carriage. "My boy, you must show the children to their rooms. Make haste," he says.

The driver pivots to scan Edgar, and immediately is consumed with an ominous feeling surrounding the new guest. Something is different about him. His eyes appear darker than before, and his complexion is pale, washed of warmth. His feet move past the child without a word, and he makes his way to the estate's entrance.

Thinking the man's behavior is odder than usual, David turns to his nephew to apologize. "You must ignore him. He must be unwell from the long journey and lack of sleep," he says as he watches Frederick continue his path to the door.

He moves to stand next to the children and smiles. "Thank God you two don't have any luggage, or else I fear he really would have crumbled." He nervously giggles, and his palms sweat. The children laugh at his joke. "All right, then, let's follow him inside to meet the staff and get you acquainted with your sleeping quarters," he says.

Before finishing the invitation, both kids link arms with one another and skip towards the front entrance.

A bit confused by Fredericks's change of character, David pauses behind. As soon as he notices the group has reached the front door, his attention returns, and with a single hop, he starts his quick-paced steps to catch up. Standing at the tail end of the group, he notices his driver fumbling for the set of keys to the house and becomes concerned at the sight of his shaking hands. "Everything okay, chap?" he asks.

Not seeming to hear him, Frederick turns the ornate skeleton key in the lock, and a loud *click* sounds to signify their readiness to enter. He opens the door with a sense of urgency and stiffly walks inside.

The open entrance reveals the grand foyer of the estate. The floor is constructed entirely of immaculately clean white marble, crisply polished, and perfectly accented by the vaulted ceilings depicting a scene of flying cherubs in a clouded blue sky.

Nervous about how the children will like their stay, David places his hand on Edgar's back. "How do you like your new home?" he asks.

The affluent scenic change leaves the young boy speechless. Taking a deep breath, he encounters the rich smells of sandalwood and lavender wafting in the air. The scents serve as an introduction to the lifestyle he was born to live, and the revelation that he is finally reaping the rewards of his birth rite creates an enormous smile on his face. He remains silent while his wide eyes soak in each detail, and the thought that one day it will all be his runs through his mind. He feels the pressure of his uncle's palm on his left shoulder and nods before he can articulate his words. "Very much so," he says.

Desiring the child's approval, the words leave David with a sense of accomplishment. "Good," he says.

As the heirs take a moment to stand in admiration of their wealth, Frederick exits the room and reenters with a group of the estate's staff. One by one, they shuffle past with their eyes diverted toward the floor as they form a line in front of the new guests. Mostly women make up the twelve-person workforce. Some work in the kitchen, and others keep the house tidy, but regardless of their assigned duties, they have one thing in common: they are each clad in matching earth-tone brown dresses and bonnets. Not a single piece of their uniforms is form-fitting, including the head coverings, making the hue of their peeping eyebrows the only way to discern their hair color.

Edgar, disinterested in introductions, scans the vaulted dome-shaped ceiling to analyze the painted group of flying cherubs. As he shifts his eyeline to each set of the angelic babies' eyes, the pit of his stomach fills with unease. His uncle's clearing throat grasps hold of his attention and distracts him from his nausea, filling him with a sense of relief. "Yes, dear uncle?" he says.

David snaps his fingers, and a woman steps forward from the lineup. Her skin is slightly more weathered than the rest, and her eyebrows are the color of day-old mustard. She sternly squints at the small boy. The uncle smiles as he points his finger in the woman's direction to introduce her. "Yes, this is Ms. Tiller; she will be the nanny in charge of your scholarly endeavors and will watch over you when I am occupied with daily business dealings," he says.

The small boy slowly studies the woman's body language from top to bottom. Her uptight demeanor is unwavering as she stares at his wandering gaze. Trying to establish dominance, she tilts her nose slightly up and opens her mouth to speak. "Good afternoon, Mr. Manley," she says.

Edgar finds the timbre of her voice to be like his mother's, and it irks a nerve. He clears his throat and, with a playful chuckle, motions to Louise. "Don't forget about Ms. Manley," he says.

Immediately, the woman finds offense at the younger boy correcting her. She refuses to look at where his finger is pointing, and her eyes remain fixated on the master of the house. Even though she is not focusing on him, the boy, in the act of intimidation, continues to glare at her face.

Attempting to regain control and de-escalate the situation, David speaks to the maid directly. "Ah, yes. With things being such a blur because of the new arrivals, I had almost forgotten to mention there is also a girl," he says.

Ms. Tiller stubbornly pivots her head, locking eyes with the boy.

Noticing no improvement in the room's tension, David swiftly steps forward, and his lips nervously quiver. "Ms. Tiller, why don't you escort the children to their rooms?" he says.

The small boy moves his pointing hand to the sky to give a command. "I assume you mean one room, since we should like to stay together. Considering everything we have been through, I'm certain your compassionate heart wouldn't find it too much of a burden to move another bed into whichever room you have chosen for me," he says.

Before the child can devise another reason for the request, David claps his hands in the air to get the attention of one of the male servants standing with perfect posture in the lineup. He calmly speaks to his nephew while waiting for the servant to rush by his side. "Of course, that is the least I can do," he says. His hand lifts to his mouth to shield anyone from reading his lips, and he leans to whisper instructions to the man beside him.

The servant gallops his way up the waterfall-shaped staircase, and his steps quicken to a full sprint as he nears the location of the children's sleeping quarters.

Having someone perform at his beck and call makes the young boy beam from ear to ear, and his expression of happiness pleases the uncle. He turns to acknowledge Edgar with a smile. "Very well, then, he shall have your request taken care of before you reach your quarters," he says. Switching his attention, he gives instructions to Ms. Tiller. "Please show them their room so they may have time to settle into their new accommodations."

As soon as he finishes the command, she glances at the boy. "Very well," she says. With a delicate clap of her hands, she starts her journey to the staircase. "Come along now, child... children."

Edgar reaches for his sister's hand. Even though she feels made unwelcome by the woman responsible for them, the smile remains plastered on her tiny lips. Giggling at one another, they hurry to catch up to the older woman.

The massive staircase is a whimsical forest-themed art piece rather than a pathway to the second floor. Its magnificent tree-like railing and waterfall-shaped steps contain black-and-white marble accents with extensive gold detail. The last step leading to the hallway narrows like the beginning of a cascading waterfall.

Pausing at the bottom, the children take a moment to appreciate the ornate detail of the gold shapes surrounding the railing's marble edge and the black baroque velvet stair runner that lays perfectly centered down the middle of each step. Their newly found wealth overjoys them.

Ms. Tiller ascends halfway up the stairs and stops. Irritated by the lack of footsteps following behind her, she refrains from looking back, but holds her right fist by her side and snaps her fingers to summon them.

Not wanting to cause a scene in front of their uncle, they keep their mouths shut and travel up the extensive steps toward the woman they despise. They almost run into the back of her still body, thinking she will continue to move.

She transitions her clenched right fist into an open hand and extends it behind her as if training puppies. For a moment, she waits for someone to grab hold, and not receiving a response, she becomes impatient. With a stern tone, her voice commands. "Edgar, take it now," she says.

He glares at her offered palm as they stand frozen on the step. He shifts his eyes toward his sister, then back to the maid, and with a clenched jaw, he quietly responds. "Miss, do not make me repeat myself. There are two of us," he says.

Having a child contradict her command makes Ms. Tiller livid, and her once-inviting hand clenches into a fist. With her eyes focused dead ahead, she addresses his complaint. "Very well, then," she says and continues up the staircase to the hallway.

Her lack of acknowledgment causes rage to form in the small boy, and before taking a single step to follow, he pivots toward his sister. "Don't worry, dear sister. Her poor treatment of you will not be tolerated, and I can assure you I will not allow it to happen again!"

With a smirk indented on her lips, she nods her head, and together, they follow behind the cranky woman.

The hallway is lined with various commissioned paintings of the Manley family in varying configurations. Some display groups, others individuals, couples, people on horseback and with pets, but they have one thing in common: Edgar pictures himself in each.

Elaborately carved gold-and-silver candle sconces assume their positions between every portrait, illuminating the intricate details of the oil paint layered on canvas. The quality is exquisite, and an up-close view gives the observer a mountain of color.

As they move through the long corridor, Edgar spots a familiar dark-featured face on the wall of portraits and quickly squeezes his grip around his sister's hand to signal for her to stop.

The painting depicts the likeness of Daniel Manley. He is wearing a similar outfit to their encounter with him in the dark alleyway. His body has a black coat tail suit, a gold-encrusted cane, and a matching black top hat. A dark golden frame perfectly encapsulates the photo.

The children remain frozen in place, admiring their father.

Noticing they are no longer following behind, Ms. Tiller turns around and sees that they have paused in front of a portrait of Daniel in young adulthood. She stops herself from demanding their obedience, and, remaining quiet, creeps up behind them. Their focus, locked on every detail, consumes their attention as she opens her mouth to break the silence. "You have his likeness," she says.

Her words put a smile on Edgar's face, and his demeanor softens. Out of his peripherals, he glimpses his sister, appearing discouraged from being left out again, and his warming interaction turns cold. "I assume you mean both of us?" he asks.

The woman responds with a cackle.

In unison, both children turn to face her. "What's so funny?" Edgar asks. Before she can answer, he continues, "I dare say we both fancy a good joke when called for. So, what is it?"

Feeling she is being disrespected, Ms. Tiller lowers herself to one knee and aligns her eyes with his. Remaining silent, she glares at him in a show of dominance.

His eyes stare directly at her pupils, and his lips form a sarcastic grin. "That is precisely what I thought," he says. Taking his sister's hand, he pulls her closer. "Now, Ms. Tiller, apologize to my sister."

As Ms. Tiller's eyes sweep beside him, she laughs. "Why should I? Not being compared to him should be of no consequence, as your father was an unusual man, and there is no reason you should want to be like him," she says.

The girl's face retains her usual smile, and the boy's expression turns sour.

Her knowledge of dampening the mood satisfies Ms. Tiller, and, wanting to knock the child down a few emotional pegs, she continues to probe. "Oh, they didn't tell you?" she asks.

Edgar's foot taps against the ground, and he becomes impatient. "Tell us what?" he asks.

Ms. Tiller smirks as she directs her attention to the portrait they had just admired. "Have you not paid any notice to you not having grandparents?" she asks. Before allowing a chance for anyone to answer, she continues. "That man you call father killed them. After that horrible instance, you should be thankful to the lord of the house for even letting you stay." She releases a huff of air as she walks away.

Feeling that she is condemning the man who has provided this lifestyle for them angers the children, and their blood seethes.

The boy lightly touches his sister's shoulder and whispers, "It will be alright, Louise. We will clear his name. I will handle this." His fingers lift the corner of his lips to instruct her to deepen her smile, and they mimic Ms. Tiller's hurried steps as they follow behind.

The trek ends at a nondescript door at the far end of the hall. Fiddling for her keys in her apron, the nanny's hand stops when it encounters what it searches for, and she withdraws a worn brass skeleton key from her pocket.

While the woman places the key in the door, the young boy asks questions regarding the situation. "What did our father do? We have not been privy to any information or accusations. We spent only a moment in his presence, and knew him very little."

The door opens with a *click* of the lock, and Ms. Tiller lets them inside. As she watches them enter, she fixates on how similar the small boy is to his father, and immediately, her mind is overtaken by his memory. "Well, he was a frigid man. Some would even say his eyes were devoid of emotion. It was almost as if his attractive outward appearance masked something evil buried within. Several shocking situations that I will refrain from speaking on involved him during his time here, but the one that many already know surrounds the last carriage ride he took with your grandparents. They perished, and he came out unscathed, the only survivor. The circumstances of their deaths were quite suspicious, and he disappeared the very night they passed. As the assigned caretaker who helped raise the unusual boy, I knew in my gut he was different, and that their demise was solely at his hands, but, in all fairness, that is just my opinion, and my thoughts hold little relevance in this estate," she says.

Irritated by her accusations, the small boy mutters under his breath, "As they shouldn't."

The older woman perks up at his voice and becomes defensive. "What did you say, child?" she asks.

He smirks. "I told my sister how brave you were for disclosing your opinion. Ms. Tiller, it would be quite beneficial if you just trust us," he says. Turning to his sister, he lifts his hand to nudge her shoulder. "Isn't that right, Louise?" She silently nods with enthusiasm.

Tired of dealing with the children's nonsense, Ms. Tiller ignores the boy's comments and rolls her eyes. As she heads for the exit, she glances back at them with a condescending smile. "I can make this stay both easy and difficult for you, boy. You have complete control in determining your fate," she says.

The children stay silent as they watch her depart the room. Upon hearing the door close, they turn to one another to laugh.

Edgar prances around the room, imitating the woman's rigid stature, and raises his voice to a high, screeching pitch. "I am a wise old troll, which gives me the right to torment children more privileged than me," he says. Louise finds his behavior comical and silently laughs with a wide-open smile.

A dark, undefined mass develops in the room's corner near the closet. Its edges sharpen as it grows taller, forming a human likeness on the interior brick wall. Edgar pinpoints its creator as the sunsets—the last ray of light beaming through the window. Illuminating his posture generates a vague, darkened outline that eerily takes after

Ms. Tiller. Finding the resemblance entertaining, his sister sits on the floor, prepared to watch the puppet show.

Even though her brother is not moving, and no sunlight remains, the shadow continues to shift positions, relaying a vital message to the children through the unusual medium. "Listen, listen, listen," a mysterious voice chants.

Edgar sits next to his sister as their eyes peel open to take in the message. The single shadow once cast by the boy's body expands into an entire murky scene, and the show carries on without his prompting. The young audience delights in the display.

The shadow maid takes a few steps towards the corner, and her body trembles at seeing an outline resembling a pair of toes. As her upper body bends over to investigate to whom they belong, a second shadow forms a door that opens in front of her, revealing the body of the creature attached to the toes. The maid's head makes an unnatural jarring motion as it turns to view the creature's face. Before the woman can thoroughly assess it, the beast lunges from the door, and its mouth unhinges over her head. With a single swift movement of its jaw, her head pops off like a cherry from a stem, and her arms flail in the air.

The shadow's graphic reenactment paints smiles on the children's faces, and they laugh and applaud. As the headless shadow figure dissipates, the little boy excitedly turns to his sister. "You know what this means, Louise?"

Wanting him to tell her, she remains quiet and shrugs.

"This means grandmother will eat her like a profiterole, just like mother! What glorious news!" Edgar says, clapping in excitement.

As Louise's smile deepens at the pleasant thought, the beastly grandmother's shadow reappears and turns to smile with them. Together, they lay beside one another on the floor while looking up at the ceiling as the memory's warmth settles inside them.

The sounds of footsteps creaking the hall floorboards cause Edgar to be transported back to his current reality. As the distant hinges of Ms. Tiller's room open down the hallway, his eyes spring open to stare at the texture of the ceiling above him. "Dear sister, it sounds like it's feeding time," he says.

Refraining from making sudden movements, they smile to themselves and listen curiously.

As Alice tosses and turns in bed, the door of her room slowly opens. At first, with darkness swimming through the air, the being entering the woman's sleeping quarters is not visible.

Like the children, the maid's quarters are in the middle row of rooms and not a corner, so only a single window enables a view of the courtyard. Through the panes of frosted glass, only the full moon provides flecks of dim lighting that showcase the cracking door.

The creature unhurriedly sticks its hand inside the narrow slit, wrapping one finger at a time around the edge of the door's wooden molding. Each speckle of moonlight reveals a new elongated digit digging its stiff nail into the floral green wallpaper that lines the walls. The knuckles protrude like blue scarabs trapped underneath its sagging, pale white skin, and purple veins run from each fingertip to its shoulders. Frostbite appears to have affected every digit, encrusting the tip of each pointed finger with the color of necrotic black.

Unaware of the being's presence, the maid soundly sleeps, and her snores become louder.

With one hand secured to the wall, the creature places its other, finger by finger, underneath. Stretching its scrawny neck, it peeks around the corner of the doorway at the sleeping woman.

A giant gray bun piled high on its head casts a slight shadow over its lidless eyes and clustered needle-like teeth. Its charred eyebrows remain emotionless, and its overly taut facial skin provides a translucent covering over the nose and exceedingly prominent cheekbones. As its nostrils lift to sniff the air, it creeps its head further inside, searching for the desired smell and only pausing to gauge the sleeping woman's movement.

Taking a long snore through her pinched nose, she rolls over to face the wall, muttering in her sleep. "I always knew he was wicked. Nasty little brat, just like his father," she mumbles.

The creature moves a naked leg inside the room; its belly follows close behind, and soon, its entire body enters. One by one, it drags each claw along the wall, ripping pieces of wallpaper as they lacerate its surface. Focused on its snack, the creature bends its arms parallel to each bare, sagging breast and positions itself on the floor like a rabbit hunting for a carrot. As it slinks across the room, the moonlight reflects off the patches of its iridescent skin and bulging spider veins.

The bed chamber, meant for a maid or governess, is small, with minimal furniture. Within a few steps, the creature reaches the side of the bed. It takes in a deep inhalation as it drools at the sight of the woman's back. Obsessed with her smell, it leans forward, and a long bead of drool drips from a gap in its clenched teeth. The string of saliva lands on the snoring woman's cheek and rolls into her mouth.

The spice of spoiled meat causes her eyes to open. Confused by where the awful taste has come from, she uses her hands to prop herself up against the headboard, and, slowly turning to scan the bed, notices a blurry, dark outline. While rubbing her eyes to get a more detailed view, she hears the bedroom door slam shut, and the figure disappears.

The combination of her poor vision and the room's lack of light makes it difficult to decipher anything not placed within a foot of her face, leaving her unaware that the creature now hangs stock-still from the ceiling above, gawping down upon her with a smile. She scans the room and, not seeing a thing, closes her eyes, assuming that it was just a nightmare.

Silently, the creature lowers itself to the level of her bed and, with a single swipe of its hand, digs its nails into the feather mattress and tears away the covers.

Flying white feathers add a snowy glimmer to the light-less air. Disoriented and confused, Ms. Tiller's eyes spring back open as she scans the darkness for the cause of the assault.

The obscured being licks its lips with its slug-like tongue and snickers as it pulls itself closer. "Cake?" it asks.

Rather than being frightened, the maid finds herself annoyed, and concludes that it must be her mother, who has vengefully returned to haunt her in her dreams. "Go away and leave me be," she mutters. Unbothered by the thought, she takes a moment to reflect, then closes her eyes and falls asleep again.

Slithering closer, the creatures sagging breasts drag along the cotton sheets, causing static crackling sounds.

It continues to whisper with an echoing lisp. "Cake?" it asks.

This time, the words penetrate her ears, and, realizing it is not a dream, her eyes dart open in a panic. Fumbling to gather her words, she squints as she tries to uncover the details of the creature's terrifying face. "Cake? Why would I have—"

Before she can finish, the creature's mouth opens like a hippo's, taking hold of the maid's entire head with a springing motion. As her arms flail, the creature's sharp teeth compress around her neck, and her head effortlessly pops off into its mouth, like a cork exiting a champagne bottle. Blood spurts from the decapitation site, and the demonic being's neck stretches like an anaconda's as it swallows her entire skull. As the oval object slowly travels to the pit of its stomach, its esophagus stretches to the thickness of veiny cellophane, leaving no mystery regarding the meal's composition.

The taste of the woman's flesh is better than cake to the creature, and its permanent smile grows wide with pleasure. Leaving the mangled corpse in bed, it reaches into the woman's neck, dipping the tip of its finger in the bodily fluid and licking the residue. It releases a satisfaction-filled belch.

A mouse runs down the hall and sounds a small squeak. The creature's sensitive ears perk up at the high-pitched noise, and it shifts its attention from its servant snack. With a relaxed pace, it lumbers towards the door. Following the wafting scent of cake, it heads down the corridor to collect each of the offerings left outside the remaining occupied room's entries.

As the children lie in their beds speculating about what has occurred, they hear the creature's footsteps trudging heavily in the hall. They smile at the sound of their abrupt stopping, and giggle as the being devours their offerings.

Remaining quiet, they turn, facing each other from their assigned twin beds, and smirk. Unable to keep their eyes open any longer, they fall asleep as the sound of the being's footsteps dissipates.

A voice speaks to them in a deep, soothing whisper from the dark corner. "Sleep tight, my children," it says.

With his eyes shut, Edgar smiles.

Chapter 5

WHO SCREAMS? WE ALL SCREAM

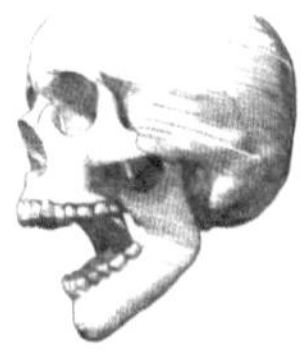

As the sun rises over the lush terrain outside, tiny beams of light enter through the estate's windows. A maid whom the children have not yet met harvests fresh eggs from the small chicken coop on the corner of the property for the house's morning breakfast. The pen's rooster projects its voice into the dense foggy air to let the brood of chickens know it is time to wake.

Unlike the innocent scene of collecting nesting chickens' eggs, the energy of the inside of the house is about to be turned upside down, and nothing will ever be the same for anyone. On the rooster's second crowing to the rising sun, countless maids start their morning routine of tidying up the sleeping quarters.

The maid in charge of laundering duties is near the age of twenty. Her braids drape from underneath her bonnet, displaying her hair's pure blonde color and length. Thankful for a place to stay and a roof over her head, she has no reason not to be joyous for her blessings and, to show it, routinely whistles as she goes through the halls collecting sheets.

While lugging a wicker basket on her hip, she makes her way to the children's room. Typically, per their routine, they start the morning upon the rooster's crow, and by the time the sun rises, they are out of bed and deep in their studies. Not wanting to wake others before they are ready, she has grown accustomed to starting with their room first to collect the sheets and make the beds.

An observant creature of habit, she has grown privy to the layout of each nook and cranny of the estate. During the first week of their stay, she noted that by the end of the rooster's call every morning, their door was left wide open, and they were nowhere in sight. She knows the home like the back of her hand and, if tasked to do so, could perform her duties efficiently blindfolded and groggy without issue, but this day is different.

After a long night of tossing and turning from bad dreams, she stumbles into the kid's closed door. The impact jolts her mind awake and causes her heart to race. Startled, she takes a moment to catch her breath and giggles at her clumsiness. She finds it abnormal that the children would still be inside, so she delicately opens the door to peer in just for precaution.

The children's bodies are under the sheets, peacefully sleeping. As one's chest raises to let out a whistling breath, the other's does the same, and vice versa.

She finds their synchronized breathing adorable. Thinking she glimpses something lingering in the children's room, she leans her upper body further through the entry to get a closer look.

A peculiarly shaped shadow sits on the edge of Edgar's bed. From a distance, it appears to be a person preparing to read a bedtime story.

Thinking the lack of sleep is catching her, the maid brushes off her curiosity regarding the shadowy figure and gives a departing glance across the room. "Sweet dreams, my little ones," she says.

As she grabs the knob to pull the door closed, she peers down and notices something on the floor by her feet. A trickle of leftover cake crumbs scatters the base of the door and into the hallway.

"Goodness gracious... I just swept you yesterday evening." Grabbing a clump of her brown servant's dress, she prepares to use it as a rag to collect the dust she believes herself to have missed.

As she lowers herself to clean the mess, she sets her wicker laundry basket on the floor beside her and sweeps the crumbles into a small pile using her dress's material.

Unlike the typical lint and dust she routinely found lingering in the hallway, the substance clings together when squished between the fabric of her skirt. She examines it with her eyes and pinches it between her fingers. "What in the world...?" she says.

While she continues to focus on playing detective, the shadow figure sitting on the bed stands, and the indentation made on the mattress returns to its normal fullness. Gradually, the shadow turns to face the partially open door.

Noticing a large crumb on the other side of the doorjamb, she sluggishly reaches to collect it. Just as her fingers cross the threshold, the door slams shut in her face, and her digits almost become a casualty.

The shock of the abrupt noise and close encounter causes her to fall back on the floor. In a daze, and confused about who could have touched the entry, she stares wide-eyed at the wood and attempts to calm her racing heart by taking deeper breaths. She closes her eyes to remove herself from the situation temporarily. "It's okay. It was probably just a draft," she says as her fear subsides.

Picking up where she left off, she continues to clean and notices a trail of crumbs leading from the children's entryway to another room down the hall.

Not remembering seeing them before, her eyeline traces where the trail ends and notices a diminishing line going underneath Ms. Tiller's room door. Since working for the Manley family, the maid has felt the older woman has always been disrespectful of her young age, and the thought that Alice could be the culprit of the scattered food makes her livid. Irritated by the mess, she becomes convinced the poor-spirited woman is setting her up, and the last thing she wants to happen is to get in trouble for someone else's carelessness. She peers down the hallway to ensure no one is around, and, leaving the basket behind, lowers her body to rest on all fours.

She hurries to the beginning of the long line of crumbs closest to the children's door. Clearing the mess is problematic; as her tiny fingers attempt to scoop the bits from the rough texture of the wooden floor, every time she gathers the crumbs into a pile, they oddly disperse as she pinches to pick them up. Losing her patience, she moves her fingers faster against the floorboards, rolling them under her hand as she tries to make them clump together.

As the sun rises, a notion of a slight whisper disrupts the stagnant morning air, and several more shadows appear in the crevasses of the long, dimly lit hallway. The non-diminishing pile of day-old crumbs taunts the maid. She rubs her finger faster against the grain of the floorboard, and the small whisper grows louder. Paranoid that the murmuring signifies the master of the house is awake and stirring in his room, she frantically cleans. Her breath shortens, and her heartbeats quicken as her worried eyes dart to each newly formed shadow. She glances down the hall, but no one is there.

Whispering voices in different pitches join in to mock the cleaning maid. "He's coming. Hurry," they say. She scrubs faster.

She feels a sharp pain in the tip of her finger. Refraining from letting out a scream, she clutches the injury and holds it closer to her eyes to assess it. A piece of splintered wood sticks out from the rubbed-raw skin. As she pulls out the needle-like splinter, blood from the small hole drips to the floor. She places the damaged digit between her lips and sucks the wound dry. The bleeding subsides, and her eyes dart back to the tidbits on the ground.

The number of sprinkled morsels has doubled, causing her pupils to grow wide with disbelief. "This can't be possible. My mind must be playing tricks on me," she says.

As she shakes her head to clear her thoughts, the whispering voices surrounding her grow louder, and she lifts her palms to her ears to block the torment. Even with the sound muffled, she can still hear them clear as day. Trying to mute them, she presses her palms harder into the sides of her head.

The pressure causes blood to build in her finger wound, and as it drips, the red coloring leaves a painted mark down her cheek. Again, her eyes dart in each direction, looking at the shadows. The voices sound shrill and mimic nails against a chalkboard, and she wants the terrifying annoyance to stop. "What do you want?" she asks.

Escalating in velocity, the multidirectional whispers join in one deafening coordinated chant. "Clean, clean, clean," they say.

As the command enters her eardrums, her pupils elongate and turn a dark, murky shade, mimicking the shadows. "I must clean," she says as her glazed eyes stare down at the floor. "I must."

The sight of the mess causes her pupils to fill the whites with the black of her irises. Her nostrils flare as they inhale the scent of the cream-colored white fragments, and she grins. The smell causes her to lick her lips and saliva to build up in the corners of her mouth. Unable to withhold her desire, she leans her upper body towards the floor and sticks her tongue out to taste the substance. The cluster of whispering voices swirls in the air, creating invisible chaos.

Her taste buds swell with a sensory overload from the sweet savories, shifting the chemistry in her brain with her addiction to the taste. Leaving her tongue against the rough wood, she moves her body closer to the floor and lies on her belly. All the clustering shadows shift towards one another to gather and watch.

She cannot contain her desire for more, and succumbs to the lure of the substance. In a smooth motion, she unnaturally bends her elbows and kneecaps in an unsettling contortion, slinking across the floor like an alligator moving over dry land to hunt its prey. As she licks up the rest of the line of crumbles, her mouth grows more expansive. Her crazed expression causes her to appear deranged, and she loses focus on her surroundings.

The group of shadows shifts in front of Ms. Tiller's closed bedroom door, and a whisper with a purring undertone calls for her.

Blinded by her desire for cake, she devours every crumb without acknowledging the droning noise. With each desperate lick, her tongue is plagued with splinters, and the friction causes open sores to form on the sensitive organ. She attempts to suck in the crumbles from under the closed door and leans in too closely, whacking her head on the wood. Her mouth hisses at the lumber blocking her addiction.

Listening to her animalistic command, the condensed shadows disperse and fall silent as the door opens with a drawn-out creak to let her inside.

Her head immediately resumes its prior position, searching for specks to consume. She follows the trail to feast, and her body continues its jarring crawl inside the room to scavenge as her tongue leaves a trail of blood on the floor, her skirt smearing the mess like a dirty rag mop.

The room lies soaked in blood that is still wet to the touch, and remnants of vanilla cake rest piled in a line leading to the bed.

Ignoring the gory scene surrounding her, the maid relentlessly follows the bait. As she comes to the end of the crumbles, her tongue savors the last bite, and her nostrils flare to sniff the air. Met with no more cake scent, the fresh aroma of iron wafts into her nostrils and knocks her out of her fixated state.

The sun has risen enough that the single window inside the room lets in the daylight, causing the shadows to dissipate. As the darkness leaves the room, her pupils shrink, and her irises return to their original shade of white. Her motor functions restore as her mind awakens.

Realizing she is on the ground, her eyes dart as she gathers her bearings. To her horror, a sullied crimson floor surrounds her, and she panics. She scrambles to sit up, regrettably aligning her eyes with the bed.

The headless corpse of Ms. Tiller lays sprawled out on her blankets. Blood-stained sheets surround her mangled body, and her skin is dry as a bone. She appears brittle to the touch.

The grotesque imagery of the scene causes the maid to go into a profound shock. Her mouth slowly opens, and her trembling hands clutch her pale white blood-stained cheeks. She frantically places her hands beside her and kicks her feet, propelling herself back towards the bedroom door to get as far away from the body as possible. The horror soaks into her subconscious, and she snaps out of her shock. She screams with all the air she can grab hold of in her lungs.

Immediately, in response to her desperate call, the door swings open inches away from the maid's back. David emerges in his nightgown, holding a loaded rifle. His shaking hands wrap tightly around the gun barrel, and his adrenaline-laced heartbeat correlates with his hyperventilating breath.

Remaining at the edge of the door frame, he witnesses the blood and gore, and his eyes widen with fear. "Jesus Christ!" he says. As his mind slides into shock, his complexion turns pale, and his hands lose grip on the gun's handle.

The gun thumps as it hits the hardwood, and the jimmied trigger causes it to shoot. Sounds of pings echo as the bullet ricochets off the brass fixtures, and David covers his ears to shield them from the noise. A woman's shriek causes him to close his eyes with a wince. His mind races with wild thoughts, convinced that he, too, has suffered an injury.

As soon as he hears the noise cease, he timidly opens his eyes to look at the horrific scene and notices the bullet has killed the young maid. Slowly, his wide eyes peer down at the still-smoking gun, then back to the freshly deceased girl. The firearm lies in a pool of blood.

Not wanting to touch the weapon anymore, he tiptoes around the smears of bodily fluids and nudges the gun with his pointed toe. A cold shudder runs down his spine as he watches it slide underneath the bed. Feeling squeamish, he stares up at the ceiling to catch his breath. He glances at the maid's open eyes and nervously lifts his hand to move toward her. "So sorry," he says.

Her dead glare offers no response.

Ill at ease over his bullet-involved indiscretion, he dodges bodily fluids as he races out of the room and screams for Frederick. As he waits for the driver to come to his rescue, he paces the hallway while devising an excellent story to clear any association with the murderous action.

The sound of heavy footsteps barreling up the staircase causes him to jump. As soon as he realizes it is just the driver responding to his call, he calms down and tries to explain.

Even though he appears to be the same physically, something is still off about Frederick. His pupils almost look lifeless and lack compassion.

David releases a puff of air from his lungs as he places a hand on the driver's shoulders. "Good, it's you." His speech is so fast that it is barely understandable. Directing him to walk, he leads him down the hall to the outside of Ms. Tiller's room. "I need you to do me a favor, and it must stay between us."

The driver nods coldly.

"Before I show you, I need to prepare you that there is a dead body behind that door. There are two, to be precise," David says as he places a quivering hand on the knob.

Frederick is unfazed by the news.

"It appears the young one may have decapitated the other, then shot herself, but of course, I wasn't in the room when it occurred, so there is no way to tell exactly what happened," David says. Twisting the knob a little more under his fingers, he continues. "So, that's where you come in. We both know how squeamish I can get around blood and how bad this endeavor will look if others in the manor find out, so I need you to clean up this mess, and no one can ever know."

Instead of acknowledging him, Frederick stares at the closed door, waiting to see inside.

The lack of response causes David to stammer. "Do you understand?" he asks.

The driver nods with a devious smirk.

"Very well, then," David says. He shoves the door open to let Frederick inside to get started. "All right, I shall leave you to it." The door quickly shuts, and he scans to see the driver has disappeared. Immediately, he is relieved the problem is being taken care of, and feels a weight lifted from his chest as he lets out a heavy sigh.

Something tugs on the back of his nightshirt. He spins around and finds both children standing directly behind him. The small boy wears a new navy-blue colored matching suit, a white ruffled shirt, and polished black loafers with golden buckles. His sister remains in the same outfit she arrived in.

As the young boy watches the adult man stumbling for words, he glances at the outfit on his sister's body and briefly explains. "I think they must have forgotten to bring Louise's new wardrobe to our room, so they forced her to wear what she came in."

The children's surprise appearance causes David to clutch his chest, bypassing the boy's concern. "You can't sneak up on a man like that! Cripes, how long have you been standing there?" he asks. Placing his hands on his knees, he slumps over to catch his breath and stop himself from having a panic attack.

Wanting confirmation of his concern, Edgar clears and sniffles his nose to get his uncle's attention.

David waves his hand. "Oh yes, I will have someone tend to that. Don't worry," he says.

The children look at him with amusement. Edgar shrugs. "Are you certain of that, dear uncle? The staff's services are quite lackluster," he says. Changing the subject, he attempts to pretend like he knows nothing, even raising the pitch of his voice to that of a three-year-old child to sound innocent. "Is everything okay? You look pale."

Edgar's comment surprises David, and he becomes paranoid that the small boy may know something. Fidgeting his fingers together, he skeptically glances back to the room of their nanny. Once he confirms the door is closed, he continues, "Oh, yes, yes. Everything is quite all right." His lips twitch with a forced smile.

The children want to distract him from asking any more questions. Staring at his casually dressed body, they giggle at the pajamas.

Feeling embarrassed, David shifts his attention to his attire and grabs the neckline of his top with his two fingers. He pulls the material away from his throat to allow air to cool his chest. "Do you find it hot in here?" he asks as his eyes anxiously dart the hallway. Before anyone can answer, he says, "Well, I was just taking a morning stroll, but the day is getting away from me, and I think it best I get changed into proper clothing." Desiring to end the conversation, he spins around and darts back to his room at the end of the hall.

The boy quietly tugs on the skirt of the little girl's dress. "Watch this, sister," he says. Clearing his throat, he raises his voice and yells to his uncle, "Is everything okay with Ms. Tiller? She didn't wake us this morning."

The words strike a nerve with David and stop him dead in his tracks. Still facing the opposite direction, his back remains towards the kids, and before he opens his mouth to speak, his hand lifts to answer the child. As he winces, covering up his lie, the memories of discovering the maid's grotesquely massacred body come back to him. Immediately, remembering the gory sight causes his face to turn green, and he fights back the urge to dry heave. In response to covering up the deep-seated sickness, his facial expression pinches together and uncomfortably tightens.

The children enjoy watching him flounder. Knowing the offering of the cake disappeared from their door frame, the children are confident their suspicion of the dead nanny is accurate and fight back a snicker.

Worried he may give away his guilt for contributing to the bloody massacre, David refrains from turning his head to answer the kids. As he prepares himself to lie, his cheeks clench, and then he yells over his shoulder. "She left early this morning and had a family emergency to attend to," he says. Taking a few steps forward, he remembers the young maid is also gone, and as he continues to walk, he yells an explanation behind him. "The young maid you see every morning straightening things up—well, I encouraged her to join Ms. Tiller for emotional support. So, they will both be absent until further notice." His flustered state gets the best of him, and he quickens his pace to his room.

The children hold their composure until they hear his door shut behind him. The siblings look at one another with excitement. As Edgar smirks, he whispers to his sister, "You hear that, Louise? That means we can do whatever we want today. No bossy nanny means no schooling and no rules."

She smiles at him. Taking her hand, he gives her palm a giant squeeze. "Shall we see what has happened?" he asks. Her smile grows more prominent, and she nods with enthusiasm.

Edgar pulls Louise behind him to the grouchy maid's bedroom door, and they lower themselves to the level of the door's keyhole to peek.

The inside of the room appears to be spotless, with Ms. Tiller's bed entirely made with fresh sheets. Oddly, there is no sign of the driver or any other life.

The sight fills them with a sense of confusion and dis-appointment, and it irritates the small boy. "How unfortunate. We appear to have missed all the fun," he says.

With a look of condolence, Louise stares into his eyes to relay a voiceless message. He shrugs. "I guess you are right, dear sister; there will be plenty more for us to see. We must keep our heads held high," he says. The children exchange a smile.

"Shall we go for a stroll through the maze outside?" Edgar asks. Louise dramatically nods. He holds out his arm for her to take, and she accepts his offer.

They sing a jolly tune as they make their way to the staircase.

Chapter 6

BLOODY MAZE

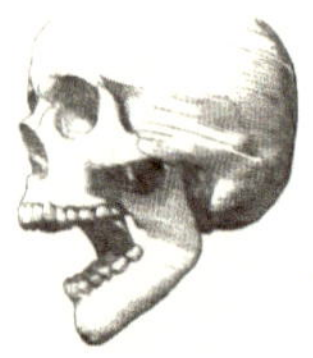

Carrying on with their day, the kids skip down the stairs to go outside to play. As the joy-filled whistling moves further down the hallway, David peeks his head around the door to see if the coast is clear. The sight of their departure gives him a sense of relief, and a deep breath vibrates through his lungs. Slowly, he retreats into the safety of his room to finish getting ready for the day.

The children chase each other outside the large front door of the estate. Louise runs from her brother, and he sprints to catch up. "You can run, but you can't hide!" he shouts. She peeks over her shoulder and giggles at him as she dashes towards the hedge walls of the maze.

Edgar's breathing grows heavy. He stops and hunches over to calm his exerted lungs and racing heart. As he glances up, he sees the material of her velvet dress flowing behind the edge of the hedge wall before vanishing into the maze. "Such a tricky little minx," he says. Wanting to win their game of tag, he follows her into the boxwood labyrinth. The lush greenery starts at the top of the kids' heads and grows taller as each row becomes closer to the center.

As Edgar wanders, he admires the vibrant colors of the green bushes and flowering vines. He only has one way to travel, so he starts down the seemingly simple path to find his sister. He hears the faint sound of a girl's laughter and picks up his pace. His head jolts from left to right to analyze the thick hedge walls and pristinely kept shrubbery for any sign of his sibling's whereabouts.

Reaching the end of the path, he has no other option but to turn left, venturing further toward the center. With an indistinct shrug, he accepts the challenge and resumes his running.

Louise's laughter becomes louder. Sneaking up on her is thrilling and fills Edgar with excitement. "I'm coming to get you!" he says.

With a sinister snicker, he is met with the option to go left or right. His hand scratches his chin as he ponders his choice. Lifting his opposite finger, he moves it back and forth like the hand of a ticking clock. "Eenie, meenie, miney, moe..." Even though his recital of the child's rhyme is unfinished, his finger freezes in its position, pointing to the left. "It appears I have chosen that direction."

As he turns to follow the path of his pointing finger, a dark presence lurks in the opposite direction. Unlike the typical comfort of the shadow, its core nature feels ice-cold, with prickling spikes of malevolence.

While whistling a merry tune, Edgar swings his arms at his sides while gazing at the sky and smiles at the sun's warmth on his cheeks. Tiny birds chirp above and sing to praise the beautiful day.

As he reaches the end of another row, he again faces a decision on which way to travel. Feeling that his father may control his guiding finger, he lifts the tip to help him choose his path. "All right, father, which way will my feet travel?" he asks as he tightly shuts his eyes. As he wags his finger side to side, waiting to see where it freezes, he thinks of how much fun his father must have had playing in the same shrubbery as a child. Still waving his digit from left to right, he experiences a rush of happiness flowing through his veins.

The harsh cawing of a large black raven shifts his thoughts, and as he comes out of his fantasy, something grabs hold of his finger. Immediately, he thinks his sister is playing a trick on him, and he chuckles. "That's not how tag works when I'm the one who is it!" he says. As his eyes slowly open, something doesn't feel right, and he pauses in moving his gaze when his eyes encounter an individual's feet.

Their wrinkled texture makes them appear as though they belong to someone seasoned. Each uncut nail curls underneath its bony, callused toes, and the skin's hue is a translucent shade of pale blue—off-white lace stained with blackened crimson dangles to the protruding ankle bones. The substance fills in the gaps of the ornate embellishment, making the eyelets look intermittently woven with a thick burgundy ribbon.

Not recognizing the bare feet causes the small boy to become curious, and he moves his pupils to keep analyzing the being's other attributes. As his eyes scan up the nightgown, they stop at its claw-gripped hands.

Clutched between its ridged fingers is a bun of graying hair attached to a severed head, which the airy breeze is slowly spinning.

Edgar patiently stares at the back of the silver accented scalp and waits for it to rotate enough to expose its identifying features. As it smoothly twirls, the face reveals itself as Ms. Tiller, making Edgar rather happy.

Her mouth is encrusted with putrid dried residue, and her shriveled skin is dehydrated to the bone. Both eyes have rolled back in the woman's skull, so only the white of each iris and burgundy veins are displayed. Underneath her nose is a mouth frozen in the position of a sinister gaping scream.

His eyes grow wide in anticipation as they travel up the rest of the grimy nightgown to the entity's neck. The skin and cartilage appear jagged from teeth tearing, rather than a ligature's clean cut.

Realizing the head belongs to the entity holding it, Edgar glances back and addresses the dangling appendage. "I dare say, Ms. Tiller, I believe this look suits you nicely," he says.

The sound of his words causes her ears to ooze a fetid substance and her jaw to tense, cracking as its petrified joints unhinge to release a guttural shriek. The child takes a step back as the low-octave pitch resonates in the air.

Ms. Tiller swings the stray head by its hair towards him, and its protruding teeth gnash at his skin. Angry at missing the bite, each unstable foot takes a slow step closer.

The little boy takes another step away, and with a smile, he waves his hands to get it to stop. "Remember, it was not me who did this to you. Maybe this is your lesson from the almighty for being less than amiable? You know what they say—karma can be a rank beast," he says.

Ignoring him, the woman continues to swing the teeth-baring head in his direction, and like a provoked snake, it continues to strike as it gets in close range. As its mouth opens again, a hacking sound exits its severed trachea, and a swarm of locusts flies out, filling the air.

Edgar's hands frantically swing with disgust as he bats the insects away from his head. "You shall eventually learn you served your necessary purpose," he says as his foot takes another giant step backward. Watching her show no sign of backing down builds panic inside his heavily beating heart.

Ms. Tiller's kneecaps tremble, and the atrophied muscle in her legs causes her balance to collapse briefly. Without hesitation, Edgar seizes the opportunity to escape as she pauses to regain her stability. Continuing to shoo away the insects, his body drastically pivots to face the opposite direction, and he takes off in a dead sprint down the maze's path.

Ms. Tiller resumes her staggering pace after him as her vertebrae re-align with one another in an upright posture. As she is about to reach the end of the row, Edgar notices a fork in the path's approach, and, wanting to assess how much time he has before her arrival, he glances over his shoulder.

The moment his head shifts to look, he runs into something. The impact causes him to bounce back, and he tumbles to the freshly trimmed grass. He quickly hops to his feet to assess his trousers for stains and finds nothing. Turning his head, he scans for what triggered his fall, and finds it was the young maid.

At first glance, even though her complexion is ghostly pale and her lips an unnatural shade of blue, he focuses on her regulation uniform and sighs with relief. "Oh, am I ever so glad to see you. A deranged woman is chasing me," he says as he points behind him. Swiftly looking at the slowly staggering beheaded woman approaching, he realizes he has some time, and cups a single hand around his mouth to relay a loud secret. "I fear something has infected her with rabies or the shingles. Either way, as you can see, she is quite unwell."

Rather than sympathizing with the child, the young maid takes on the expression of a Cheshire cat and takes a step closer. Still wrapped up in his drama, Edgar doesn't take the time to notice anything bizarre about her appearance, and becomes angry at her lack of responsiveness. "Didn't you hear me?" he asks. As she takes another step closer, he spots a bloodstain on her dress's dark-colored brown bodice, and as his eyes squint to see the cause, he notices a gunshot wound to her chest.

Muffled buzzing sounds circulate through the air, her mouth hinges open leisurely, and she moans, releasing a swarm of locusts in the child's direction. He frantically swats the space around his mouth and ears to keep them away. "Bloody hell! You are making quite the introduction," he says.

A devious grin comes across her face as she tilts her chin down, and a low, demonic growl stems from her throat. It is clear from the look of thirst in her eyes that she is not interested in helping the child.

Besides her odd behavior, Edgar finds the fact of her coming back from the dead slightly disturbing. "Well, I'd best get back to my game. I am sure my dear sister is missing me," he says. His feet shuffle underneath him, and bolting in the opposite direction to get around her allows him to escape.

Without looking back, he sprints through the maze. Even though his breath is running thin, turn by turn, he finds his way to the center. In the middle of the tricky formations of shrubbery sits a large two-tiered stone fountain and four matching stone benches for one to sit and admire its serenity.

As he takes a moment to catch his breath, Edgar hears water splashing, and his eyes dart across the open circle to glance at the source.

Louise casually runs the tip of her fingers through the water to create a rippling effect. The mesmerizing pattern of the small waves distracts her as they crash into one another.

Having just been through hell, the sight of her mundane behavior strikes a chord in the small boy's bones. He immediately becomes envious of her relaxed demeanor, and his blood boils with anger. His fists clench by his side, and he moves in an intentional marching pattern towards her. The soft grass mutes the sound of his stomps.

Stuck in a whimsical musing, Louise continues to enjoy her moment with the intriguing pool of water. Mesmerized by the feeling, she dazedly leans forward to get a more detailed look at the reflection staring back at her.

Edgar's irritation continues to build. Seizing the opportunity of her distraction, he lunges at her and, grabbing hold of the hair on the back of her head, pushes her face into the water. As he watches her air bubbles escape from every angle, he smirks at her flailing hands attempting to fight him off. "Where were you? Where were you when those bloody corpses tried to attack me?" he asks as he pushes her into the water with more force.

Her arms lose their strength as the oxygen continues to leave her body.

After waiting until the last moment possible, Edgar releases the back of her head and lets her fall to the ground. He chuckles and steps toward her as she hacks up water from her lungs. "Don't be a baby, dear sister," he says as he offers his hand to help her up.

She struggles to regain her breath while looking at him with suspicion. He extends his hand further for her to grab. "Come, now. You know I was joking and would never hurt you."

She wraps her trembling hand around his with a meek smile and stands. "I know," she says as she avoids eye contact.

Her remark stuns him, and his eyes open wide. In shock from her words, he stammers. "L-L-Louise! You spoke..."

His look of surprise causes her to giggle. "Of course I did. I'm not mute," she says as she takes hold of her dress to dry her face.

He rushes to her to apologize. "Yes, I know. I just was uncertain if this day would come," he says, wrapping his arm around her shoulder.

Reading into his deceptive mannerisms, Louise uses her fingers to brush his arm off her. As she clears her throat, her words form together like those of a stroke victim regaining their speech. Her feet move back to the large fountain basin, and she redirects his attention by pointing to the top. "Did you notice the statue above?" she asks.

Immediately, Edgar's eyes drift to the area she is referencing. The statue matches the rest of the swirled marble stone, but unlike the fountain, the surface has no wear. The sculpture is of an angelic child playing a horn to the heavens, and the face resembles the boys.

"This must be the statue they promised you, dear brother," she says.

Unhappy with his characterization, Edgar moves to stand beside her and profoundly analyzes the carved details. He shrugs. "It is rather hard to tell," he says. Taking a pause, his posture stiffens, and he turns away. "Maybe our uncle was referring to a different one."

She finds his annoyance entertaining, and, realizing how bothered he is, she continues. "No, I must confess—it bears quite a likeness to you. Dare I say that if you stood beside it, I may well not identify one from the other," she says.

Edgar's loving facade becomes harder to maintain as his anger takes over. Knowing he must keep his composure, he races to the center of the space. As he turns to summon his sister, the shrubbery rustles behind him, and the noise makes him jump. The fear of both zombies coming to get him makes his body freeze.

At once, he lifts his finger and locks out his elbow to point at his sister. "She's the one you are after," he says.

Her facial expression goes sour, and she glares at him. She yells to contradict his words, "He is the one you want!"

The figure turns the corner, revealing itself as Frederick. The pants of his driver's uniform are dirt-smudged, and his hands are grass-stained. Before anyone can address him, Edgar puts on a show to gain his sympathy. Gazing up at him, he exhales a massive sigh of relief. "Hello, dear friend," he says.

Ignoring his greeting, Frederick snaps at the child. "What are you doing out of the house?" he asks.

Unaware of how much the driver knows about the early-morning events, the small boy bides his time to devise a response. As he ponders his next move, he notices Frederick's uncharacteristically disheveled appearance and the suspicious stains. "Are you hiding a secret?" he asks.

Exhausted by his day's tasks and at his wit's end, the driver lets out a huff and rolls his eyes. "I was told to retrieve you for breakfast," he says.

The boy puts on a smile. "That is excellent because I, for one, am starving," he says.

Without saying another word, Frederick spins around and starts his departure from the maze.

Louise clears her throat, catching Edgar's attention, and he glares daggers to stop her, bulging his eyes. They glance back and forth at one another with varying expressions as each tries to rival the other's dominance. The small boy lifts a finger to his throat and pretends to slit it, and wanting to keep her life, Louise stops the battle and remains expressionless.

Edgar extends his hand for her to take. "Come along now, sister. Let us go as one," he says. His impatience shows through his snapping fingertips as he summons her to move faster.

As she runs to take his hand, Louise hears whispers travel around the fountain from the shadows cast by the sun against the hedged walls. Even though the rhetoric of jargon is nondescript, the message causes her eyes to widen, and she gulps.

Edgar playfully squeezes her hand. "Do not fret, sister; you know I will always care for you," he says.

They follow hand-in-hand, skipping to catch up to Frederick. As they exit the maze, Edgar glances over his shoulder and sees the two mangled servants waving at him from the hedge's shadowed entrance.

Confident in his control over the situation, he blows them a kiss. "Good riddance, hags," he says, then races to the estate.

Frederick stands waiting for them in the foyer. Though his facial expression is stone-cold, the corners of his lips contradict the severity of the notion. Without saying a word, he makes languid eye contact with the children, then turns his back for them to follow. Together, they make their way across the large foyer and past the stair-case to the dining room.

Each morning, they serve the children an average spread of pastries and teacakes. Unlike prior times, this day is different. The large, dark wooden table displays trays of meats, desserts, and scones as if they've set it for a special occasion or holiday.

David sits in the furthest seat away from the arched entryway, patiently waiting. As the driver continues into the room and moves towards the head of the house, the children stand under the dining room's archway in awe of the food aesthetically laid out before them.

David sits poised with an underlying splash of dishevelment. A tie hangs loosely around his neck, and the buttons on his shirt underneath his black-tailed jacket are unevenly buttoned. He hears the driver's heavy footsteps approaching, but attempts to avoid them for as long as possible. His stark-white face focuses on a bunch of plum-hued grapes that cascade over the edge of a silver platter holding a variety of fruit.

As he moves beside him, the carriage driver has no sympathy for his master's shaken state. Not receiving eye contact, he clears his throat and kneels beside his employer to have a private conversation. David's head leans slightly towards his driver's lips to listen, but his vision remains fixated on the plump pile of grapes.

Frederick lowers his voice to a whisper that matches the volume of the crackling flames of the candles lit on the dining-room table display. "I did what you asked and have taken care of everything."

The words ease a small portion of David's building internal turmoil, and with relief, he tilts his head a little more to acknowledge the driver. A slight smirk stretches across his lips. "Very good," he says. With a slight nod, he glances down at the dirt smudges on the man's typically meticulous pants, and his eyebrow lifts. "Where?" he asks.

Without an ounce of hesitation, the driver immediately answers. "Under the hedge on the backside of the fountain."

David briefly analyzes the boy's blank face as he waits at the room's entrance, then returns to the driver. "Did anyone see?" he asks.

The driver releases a low chuckle. "The child was a little suspicious, but I suspect the recent addition of his statue to the fountain gave him just enough of a distraction," he says.

"Good. That is what I like to hear," David says as he peers back toward the children.

The children look at one another and wonder what the grown men are whispering about. Raising his voice, David shifts his demeanor and energetically beckons them. "Don't be shy! Take a seat. We have much to talk about." He points to the two set places on either side of him at the table, and they hurry inside and take a seat.

Cream-colored napkins monogrammed with their hand-sewn initials sit neatly folded into swan shapes in front of their plates. The excitement in David's eyes builds as he waits to see their reaction to the special touch. "See, there is one for each one of you! It is quite a fantastic addition to the table," he says. As the children inspect their napkins, he motions towards the driver's stained clothing. "Frederick made me aware that you discovered your newly erected statue. As you can see, Frederick's pants sacrificed their cleanliness for your remembrance."

The children are happy with their acknowledgment and treatment. Edgar is especially pleased they are warming up to Louise.

Edgar gives Frederick a once-over. "You are such a sneaky devil. At first, I was a bit puzzled by your disheveled state, but now, the stains on your pants and your filthy hands make perfect sense," he says. As he returns his attention to his uncle, he shields his lips from the view of the help and laughs at his impending joke. "With his secretiveness, you would have thought the old chap had been digging a grave."

His uncle loudly gulps, grabs the chalice of wine in front of his plate, and chugs a large swig of the liquid. He neurotically laughs at the accusation. The little boy raises his eyebrow at his odd behavior.

Motioning to his throat, David explains. "I must apologize for my improper manners. I was rather thirsty. Sometimes, the draft in these large rooms causes my throat to dry," he says. "Edgar, you have quite the wit. What a silly thought." His head turns to the eavesdropping driver, and he laughs again. "Dear Frederick—he thought the act of burying a body possibly caused your stains."

The driver opens his mouth, and a delayed, deep laugh escapes from his gut. Together, the two grown men laugh in unison. A tear rolls down David's cheek, and he reaches for his monogrammed napkin to wipe it.

Thinking their behavior to be entertaining, Edgar joins in with an overdone laugh. "I know us children can have wild imaginations," he says.

Their uncle calms his rolling laughter and directs the help to leave the room to give them privacy, and while the driver and other servants exit, David shares undivided eye contact with the boy to respond. "Indeed," he says.

Noticing the driver leaving with the others prompts the boy's head to turn towards him quickly to add the last word. "Thank you, Frederick. It is a beautiful piece of art that I will cherish forever."

With a devilish twinkle in his eye, Frederick turns to face the child and smirks before exiting the room.

Everyone sits in silence around the table. They wait until the last maid has left the premises. Then, David shifts his body weight in his seat and places his elbows on the table. A pained smile forms on his lips as he gets ready to speak. "Go ahead now, dig into the feast," he says.

Together, the children flood their plates with cakes and meats. As they take their first bites, David seizes the opportunity to begin a serious discussion. "Since your nanny left to tend to her family, and we are uncertain of her return, I have been searching since the early morning for another nanny to provide your education," he says.

The kids exchange a smile of contentment and take another nibble of treats.

David continues. "It was a difficult and exhausting search to locate Ms. Tiller for the position. That said, I believe it will be near-impossible to locate another in a timely fashion. Based on my inquiries this morning, locating someone to take her place within the year may prove impossible."

The children's pupils grow wide with anticipation.

"Education is of the utmost importance, and I have decided that with all this disruption, it may be the best to enroll you in a boarding school," David says. He takes a large gulp of wine and wipes a drop of sweat from his nose. "I have never been to one myself, but I have heard from others that they provide a lovely childhood experience."

In unison, both siblings drop the cake from their hands to their plates. The little boy turns slowly with his mouth gaping open toward his uncle. "What if we don't want to go?" he asks.

The uncle had not prepared for a rebuttal and actively takes a moment of silence to ponder the question. As he searches for the best reply, he releases a huff of air to gain his voice. Before addressing the waiting children, his eyes falsely study the grain of the wooden table while quietly mumbling to himself. "Well, I suppose this is the moment where I am to assert my authority," he says.

Shifting his gaze to the flame of a nearby candle, he regains his focus. Staring directly at the boy's disapproving expression, he continues. "If that is what I feel is best for developing your education, then that is what you shall do. No ifs, ands, or buts. You must go to boarding school."

Immediately, the boy's gaping mouth shifts to a scowl.

With everything going wrong leading up to this moment, the sense of being in control of a single situation causes David to straighten in his seat and have confidence to fill his core. "Yes, you shall listen and respect my decision. It is firm, " he says.

As their uncle continues on a tangent about his power, the small boy leans over to his sister to hiss. "What do you think, Louise? Shall we let grandmother take him?" he asks.

She gives a coy smile. "Not yet," she says.

Her disagreeable words ruin Edgar's happiness, and his expression falls flat. "Why, dear sister?" he asks.

While awaiting an answer, his uncle raises his voice to speak louder. "With all that being said, I am responsible for making the best decisions for you, and we must make up for your prior living situation's disregard for schooling."

Picking up a small, dull butter knife from the table, he lightly clinks it against his wineglass to summon the staff. As they arrive, he instructs a server to fetch champagne for everyone. She returns with a silver tray of filled fluted glasses, and David calls on his entire staff, regardless of status, to grab one for a toast. "Let us raise our glasses in honor of our dear child's last days in our care. He will leave us for boarding school next week." His hand gently sets the knife down and joins the others in raising a glass.

The children refuse to take part in the celebration. While idle chatter and gossip distract the adults, the small girl quickly snatches pieces of the dessert to hide in her socks.

Edgar stands on the cushion of his chair. Pivoting to face his uncle, he raises his hands toward the ceiling to gather everyone's attention and stomps his feet. "You must not have heard me. We do not want to go," he says.

The uncle scrambles to his feet with embarrassment and forces him to sit in his seat properly. "Unruly child! I am now the parent, and you are my ward. This is my home, and I make all the rules in this household. You have no choice but to obey them."

Immediately, Edgar crosses his arms to challenge his uncle's authority. "Says who?" he asks as he addresses the audience in the room. "You are merely an uncle, not our father. Since our father is no longer available, I am the only man in our family who decides for my sister and me!"

In disbelief over the child's atrocious disrespect, the staff holds back their snickers and silently watches to see what will happen next. David, nervous over the room of staring eyes, clears his throat to regain control. "Boy, I will not stand for this disrespect in my house. After everything I have done for you, you will do as I say."

Looking at his uncle, the child squints to show his dismay. "But—" he says.

Not wanting to hear anymore, David cuts off the child's speech. "On second thought, your blatant disregard for my generosity has wavered my opinion," he says.

The small boy happily bounces from his chair to sit next to his sister. His small hand nudges her knee underneath the table, and he quietly whispers to her, "See Louise? We shall prevail."

David lifts his glass higher to address the room. "Everyone, please lift your glasses in a toast for these two. Cheers," he says.

Like clockwork, one member of the kitchen staff rushes through a hidden door with a newly opened bottle to refill everyone's champagne flutes. Each frantically accepts the fresh pour, obeying their boss's orders.

The children are overwhelmed with excitement at hearing the change of trajectory.

Their uncle quickly scans to verify that everyone has a full cup in hand, then continues his announcement. "Let us celebrate young Edgar's new journey to manhood. He shall now leave for his adventure in three days," he says. With an enormous smile, he ignores his reactions and takes a large gulp.

While everyone sips their cocktails, the small boy clenches his fists under the table. It is not a moment of celebration for him. He can only think about how his uncle seems to include only him in the preposterous punishment, and not his sister. His face exudes a shade of red to match his internally building anger, and his teeth grind together. "What about my sister?" he asks.

Caught up in his moment of power and celebration, the uncle ignores him, laughing while sipping his wine with the staff. Livid over the lack of attention, Edgar speaks louder through his tight-laced jaw. "I said, dear uncle, what about my sister?" he asks.

Everyone in the room falls silent. The uncle, buzzed from the flowing alcohol in his cup, lifts his shoulders in a carefree shrug, then inappropriately laughs at the child's inquisition. As the small boy's expression grows more irritated, David takes another sip. "I suppose that means she can stay here," he says. He scans the room to see everyone's expressions and finds comfort in the mutual cackles.

Edgar sneers at the room's occupants. "Why am I being punished and not her?"

"Well," David says as he thinks of a quick-witted response, "I guess that is because she is as quiet as a church mouse."

In the middle of throwing his tantrum, Edgar's mouth lets out a growling screech. "That's not fair!" he shouts as he glares at his smirking sister. Tortured by the room's mockery, he covers his ears to escape the boisterous sound. "Stop it!"

His flustered state causes the room to spin with heckling faces as he yells. Each face distorts to look like a garden of misshaped squash, and their funny appearances make him livid. "I said stop!"

Overcome by the opportunity to partake in a feast with their employer, the staff ignores Edgar's plea and continues eating, drinking, and chatting. As he attempts to calm his seething anger, he fixates his tearing eyes on the flakes of a crescent roll on the table. While his vision and focus tunnel toward the pastry, he senses a shadow growing in the room.

Behind the gathering staff's backs, a non-provoked shadow infiltrates the corner at a quickly growing pace. Continuing to consume alcohol, the staff members are unaware of the room's shifting temperature and brightness.

Little by little, the dining room becomes dimmer, and the ends of the small boy's lips curl. He mutters under his breath, "Hello, old friend." A deep laugh that only he can hear rings in his ears.

Simultaneously, the door to the kitchen flies opens, and the small boy perks up at the sound. Unlike last time, an unfamiliar kitchen staff member enters the room with new glasses containing another round of champagne. Even though the room's dimming light hides the individual's facial characteristics, Edgar observes the movement of ruffles lining the bottom of the woman's brown skirt, and something about the unrecognizable individual's gait seems familiar.

The server's head remains tipped down, and their eyes are focused on the floor ahead of the silver tray carrying the glasses. Ignoring everyone's chaos, Edgar squints to see if he can reveal the identity of the features poking out from underneath her oversized bonnet.

All the trivial house staff takes the newly offered drinks from the tray, but before David and Frederick can summon one for themselves, the individual hurries out of the room. His uncle brushes off the lack of service and pours himself more wine from the table. As the room's occupants converse, they chug their drinks.

Noticing everyone's distraction, the small boy quickly excuses himself from the table to follow the mysterious woman. His sister stays seated to avoid causing more suspicion among the others.

Bobbing through the weaving legs and flailing storytelling arms, Edgar carefully dodges the drinking group as he makes his way to the kitchen door. Everyone remains fixated on their conversations, and his movement goes unnoticed. Seeing nothing holding him back, his curiosity gets the best of him, and he quietly cracks the door open to peer onto the other side to better look at the server.

The kitchen is pitch-black, and the tiny sliver of light escaping from the cracked door provides the only means of illumination for the small boy's eyes. Slowly, the ray of dim light lands on top of the hunched-over spine of a squatting body wearing the same outfit he had just seen the individual wearing to serve the last round of cocktails.

The person hovers over something near a rack of pans and then suddenly squats lower to the floor.

Not being able to see the extent of the being's odd behavior irritates the boy, and he opens the door a little more to get a better look. A subtle creak sounds from the door's hinge, and the maid hears it and jolts up to listen.

Worried she might see him, Edgar slowly shuts the door enough for only one of his wide eyes to peek.

The maid's upper body turns leisurely to follow the vibration of the noise. As the eyes of the individual lift, revealing the servant's identity, the revelation causes Edgar to cover his mouth to prevent a gasp from leaving his lungs.

It is the face of his father, Daniel. The sight of his son creates a wide smirk, revealing his blood-soaked teeth. Slowly, he lifts the object in his arms towards the peeping boy's stare.

Still processing that it's his father wearing the maid's clothing, Edgar's eyes drift down from the man's bloody chin to see the offering in his hands. It is the limp corpse of the server in charge of pouring champagne.

Her throat oozes blood from the jagged marks made by sharpened, gnawing teeth, and crimson drapes her body like a custom-made gown.

As the boy slowly shuts the door, he is filled with a deep sense of satisfaction, and Daniel returns to eating.

The sound of bodies hitting the floor suddenly startles Edgar. Quickly turning, he encounters everyone who had guzzled the new round of drinks, now frothing at the mouth and seizing on the ground. His eyes grow wide, and he glances at his sister in disbelief. They share mischievous grins at one another as he rushes to take his seat. "Oh, dear," he sarcastically whispers.

Realizing what is happening, his uncle frantically scans the room in horror. "Bloody hell, this must be a joke," he says. Frederick immediately appears next to him before his mouth can release the word, "Help." A pale white shade returns to his face as he fights, becoming sick from the ghastly view and wafting smells of death. In a state of shock, his eyes fixate on his cup with paranoia.

The driver quickly helps him to his feet. "You look unwell, sir. Let's get you to your room to rest. Don't worry; I will take care of everything," he says as he ushers David from the table.

As soon as they leave, the children look at one another and break out in a fit of laughter. Edgar scans the room full of convulsing bodies. "This means war, dear sister. They will never separate us," he says.

They find comfort in the final gasping breaths of the dying bodies scattered on the floor, and each takes a piece of cake in hand to celebrate. While looking into one another's eyes, they happily laugh as they enjoy their dessert together.

Licking the crumbs from his lips, Edgar gives a devious smirk. "They may need a bigger maze," he says.

Chapter 7

HE MUST GO

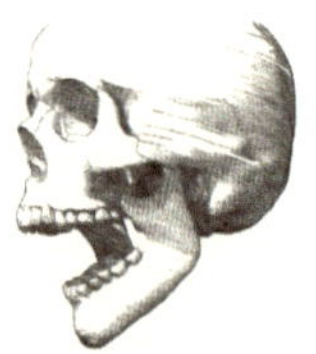

As night falls on the estate, everything appears darker than the previous nights, both literally and figuratively. Since the morning extravaganza, the new lack of helping hands has caused a simulated eclipse within the household. Only a few individuals remain inside the large mansion, and with their added duties, there is not enough time to light the home's plethora of candles, so only a handful burn in the most routinely used paths.

Immediately upon leaving the brunch festivities, the remaining staff advises the children that, for the time being, they will dine alone within the confines of their shared room.

With the limited staff available for services, everyone has found the menu for the rest of the day relatively minimal compared to previous times. They are primarily composed of food leftover from the extravagant morning buffet.

At first, the children had believed the loss of the nanny would be a positive change, but now, they experience additional confinement rather than the expected freedom. After Ms. Tiller's departure, everything had shifted their once-optimistic outlook, beginning with the morning breakfast. They find their new routine boring, and there is no one to help them around the large estate. Since neither are tall enough to reach the wall-mounted candles, their inability to light a path for exploring limits their fun, and for the first time since their arrival, both children are in their room while the sunset is on the horizon.

Edgar uses the moonlight as a source of lighting to collect his thoughts. Although hours have passed since the news of his departure to boarding school, he still stews over the verdict. With each lap, his march became more aggressive than the last. As his feet pace the room, his sister sits on the edge of her bed, intently watching his shifting mood. "How is it, dear sister, that we leave one shit hole just to have our new prosperous life ripped away like a bandage from a wound?" he says.

Sitting on the edge of the bed, Louise's feet don't touch the ground, and to distract herself from her brother's ranting, she kicks them through the air to pass the time. She adjusts herself to sit on top of her hands and shrugs.

After waiting a moment for a response, Edgar throws his hands up into the air and lets out a grunt. "If there is a time for you to speak, it is now! This is serious," he says.

She clears her throat, and as she parts her pink lips, her throat lets out a single squeak.

Edgar loses patience and flails his hands in the air for her to stop. "Never mind," he says. "I can figure this out on my own." His feet pace faster than before. As he spins his body to face the other direction, his eyes capture the moonlight's reflection, exposing his unhinged nature.

Louise mumbles under her breath. Not paying attention to her, a brilliant idea comes to the forefront of Edgar's mind, and spontaneously, he snatches his hat from the top of his head. He throws it across the room like a Frisbee. "Eureka! Brilliant!" he says.

The hard-felt brim hitting the wall causes his sister to jump. Feeling a jolt of energy from the adrenaline rush, she perks up. As she opens her mouth to inquire, he talks over her, and her eyes drop to the floor.

He spins his cane in the air like a baton and paces. Stopping his pacing, he turns around to face his sister and points the cane in her direction. "We must let grandmother have him," he says, chuckling at how long it took him to gather his conclusion. "If we remove him from the equation, they will never separate us."

Unable to hold her tongue, Louise speaks up. "But he's been nothing but nice to us," she says.

Edgar's eyes shift to glare at her. "How?" he asks.

She scoots closer to the bed's end and anxiously scans the room. "Well, he gave us this life," she says.

Edgar boastfully laughs at her statement. "You mean our dear father gave us this life," he says. The rebuttal causes her to become irritated. Having not seen this side of her, he is immediately put off by her behavior. "Don't be irrational," he says as he moves to the window to regard the moonlit sky. "We do not get what we want. We get what we deserve."

His fingers lightly trace the full moon's reflection in the glass. "You understand?" he asks. She turns away. Realizing that he is not getting through to her, he goes on with his explanation. "Every tragic event we have encountered is preparing us for a bigger purpose—something great," he says.

Her eyes flutter at the thought of more people dying at their hands, and she hastily thinks of a way to save the man who has taken care of them. "I don't believe we should get rid of David yet," she says. Quickly, she points in the closet's direction. "He hasn't even had time to tend to my new wardrobe."

Again, Edgar stares back out the window to think. "I suppose you have a point," he says. "We can keep him around for a bit longer, but we must get rid of him before I leave for that school prison."

Louise smirks. Edgar feels slightly suspicious over her protection of the uncle as he stares at the shadows engulfing the room. "Remember your place, sister. I would hate for you to upset the dear spirits who have guided us on our journey thus far," he says, while snake-like hisses stem from the room's darkened corner.

Her body fills with an odd sensation. As the hissing grows louder in her ears, an unbearable ache takes over her calf bones, and her delicate skin ripples. Terrified that something may happen to her saved offerings, she bends forward to grab the pieces of cake hidden inside her frilly socks and sets them safely beside her on the bed. A breeze blows through the sealed-off room, stirring up the smell of must.

As she takes a deep inhale to sort out her panic, the aching sensation in her legs turns into a brutal stabbing pain that quickly becomes unbearable as both her calf bones bend at an unnatural angle. Even though no movement occurs at her knee joints, her toes raise towards the ceiling. The movement causes hairline fractures to spread through her healthy bones. Her face twitches at each sound, which emulates popping popcorn.

Ignoring her agony, her brother continues to admire the moon through the leaded-glass panes. "You must choose your alliance carefully," he says.

Louise watches in horror, overtaken by a rush of anxiety as the bones in her bending limbs slink like serpents. At the base of her frilled socks, the skin on her toes tears open to form a mouth, and the tops of her feet snap to create ridged noses with eyes.

The shadows surrounding the bed creep closer. A single whisper hisses to match the snake, then more snarling sounds join in. As the sounds become overwhelming, the air thickens with the musty scent of a wormhole-riddled coffin.

Louise's pattern of breathing quickens, and she hyperventilates. "Stop!" she shouts.

Edgar smirks at her plea.

The bone-warping motion stops as Louise flails her legs, and all the shadows retract. As her toes return to normal, she scowls at the back of her brother's head. "Fine. The night before you leave, we will let Grandmother have him."

Slowly, he turns to face her with a sense of achievement. "Perfect. Great minds think alike," he says.

Unable to hold a grudge, she allows her firm demeanor to crack. Hopping off the bed, she grabs the cake stash as they share their moment of unity. "Well, I better get to it, then," she says.

Edgar nods in approval and turns around to look out the window while he waits for her to complete her evening ritual.

Louise carelessly rushes out the door with the cake pieces in her tight grip. Once in the dark corridor, she stops and quietly catches her breath. An ice-cold breeze rolls through the hall, causing a chill to run down her spine, and her body trembles. The sensation creates a feeling of unease in her gut.

Wanting to get through her cake-distribution duty expeditiously, she sets down the first small piece outside their door, and, keeping on her toes, she runs down the hall to the other two occupied rooms. The hall seems longer and narrower than before.

Unbeknownst to her, the eyes of each picture of the family's descendants shift in the lightless hall, following her movement.

Feeling like someone is watching, she twists her head from side to side to check her surroundings, and her gaze lands on the portrait of Daniel.

The once-pristine painting appears as if the layers of brush strokes are melting like the wax of a dripping candle, pooling paint at the bottom of the frame. Oddly, Daniel's white irises and pitch-black pupils remain perfectly intact as distortion occurs around them. Each liquefied area of flesh reveals a bit of bone from his skeleton. As paint runs from his face, oozing pus joins the excretions, making an iron-smelling sludge that streams down the wall. The smile on the portrait's face grows, causing each tooth to decay and tumble from the frame. A discolored, yellowing molar falls to the floor, and the ancient tooth rolls like a single die across the wooden planks, creating an eerie echo that builds nervous anticipation.

Louise evades eye contact with the portraits by staring straight ahead at her uncle's door. Her heart races faster, matching the pulses of adrenaline rushing through her veins. She lunges forward, trying to get to her destination quickly while avoiding catching sight of the old maid's door, but a light fluttering underneath the taunting wood stops her. No matter how hard she tries to circumvent looking at the flickering light, she feels her steps drawn towards it like a moth to a flame.

Without prompting, her eyes respond to the summons with a quick look. Though she is far from the woman's entry, she can feel the light warm the sockets of her eyes, and a burning sensation ensues. To eliminate the pain, she tightly closes her lids to break the spell. The act of insubordination causes her throat to tighten, and the squeezing sensation overtakes her with the pain of reliving the nanny's decapitation.

She gets woozy as it becomes harder to breathe, compromising her senses. Focusing on the shadow's torment, she feels a stabbing pain in the bottom of her foot, and the instantaneous agony causes her to stop. Unable to see what she has stepped on, she uses her free hand to feel the bottom of her appendage, trembling as she realizes the cause may be the sharp edges of the decayed molar.

Although she doesn't know what nasty turn lies ahead, she will do whatever it takes to aid the man who gave her nothing but help.

As she pulls the deeply embedded tooth from her foot, her mouth drops open to scream, but an icy hand immediately covers it, stopping the sound. In utter dismay and unable to advance, she chucks a meager piece of cake toward the uncle's closed bedroom door. Having routinely found her way through the dark hallway each night to deliver the offerings, she hopes the throw's trajectory lands the cake in its rightful place.

The few crumbles remaining in her tiny grip tumble to the floor as a nearby door opens, and something grabs and drags her into the room. Whatever the outcome for her, she wants to ensure that their grandmother isn't the reason for her demise.

Unknowingly, as David drunkenly sleeps inside his room's confines, small crumbles of cream-colored cake are scattered in front of his door for protection. Even though he wasn't aware why his fondness would grow after that moment for the young girl, he would forever have a karmic soft spot for her after her risk in saving his life.

Louise's body's movement stops, and the individual who smuggled her from the hall drops her to the floor. As she uses her arms to catch herself, she feels the same heat she had felt deep in her eye sockets engulf her body. Not wanting to address her captor, she keeps her eyes shut.

The hinges release a creak as the mysterious individual carefully shuts the entrance. After the faint click of the closing door sounds, everything falls silent around her. Thinking her captor has locked her inside and left, she focuses on remaining calm, and slowly allows her eyes to open.

A handful of burning wicks dimly light the edges of the pitch-black room. Standing ominously in the near darkness is a man holding a thin stick of wax with a flickering flame reflecting in his eyes. He stares directly into her soul; his pupils are blacker than the night outside. As she orients herself to assess the risk of the situation, she stays silent, peering into his unblinking stare.

The subtle bounces of the flame highlight a few dark burgundy stains on the floorboards underneath them. Her curious eyes look at each marked piece of wood with skepticism.

The man deliberately lifts the candle to draw attention away from the off-putting smudges. She follows the path of the dim, warm lighting back to his bloodshot eyes. Timidly, she opens her mouth to speak. "Frederick?" she asks.

His lips release a chuckle. "In the flesh," he says. Both of his pupils twinkle with an essence of aggression.

She refrains from engaging in further conversation. The shift in his eyes concerns her.

As she takes in a shallow breath to scream, he continues. "I did not intend to hurt you, child, but if you pull a stunt like that again, I may have to retract my promise," he says.

Her mouth quickly shuts. Witnessing his control over her makes him smirk in the darkness. "Much better," he says.

Both of her pupils dart around the room to decipher the identity of any vague outlines. "What do you want?" she asks as her sight lands on something in the corner. A group of tall silhouettes fills the space with muddled shapes that vaguely resemble disjointed, unclothed human frames.

He checks behind his back to acknowledge what distracts her, and the figures meet his gaze. His hand lifts leisurely, and each of his fingers wiggles to wave.

One by one, each of the dark entities awakens from their slumber. Their glowing eyes have no pupils, and as their mouths open, thin spindly teeth glow in the night.

Frederick's line of sight turns back to the girl. "You mean, what do *we* want?" he says with a smile.

She inhales a deep gulp of air and averts her eyes to avoid catching sight of the mismatched bodies. Before she can say a word, he carries on with the conversation. "Since you are at a loss for words, I will do the honor of making our message clear," he says. He leans closer to the girl, and his voice becomes softer. As he speaks, each breath briefly dims the flickering light. "You already know what we are thinking. The same thought is buried deep inside that little chest of yours. We want him gone."

Louise skims the room, catches another glimpse of the shadowy figures, and witnesses their teeth turning sinister in shape and size. "Why? He is the chosen one, not me," she asks.

The shadow causes Frederick's pupils to grow wider, taking over the whites. He is a vessel for the dark beast's message, and the shift in his vocal quality makes that clear. "The boy is trying to get rid of you, my precious child. Don't you see? He doesn't care about you. He only likes that he can control you," he says.

Louise finds her loyalty pulled in different directions as she carefully thinks through his words. "I wouldn't be here without him," she says.

"Is that what he told you?" he asks.

She shrugs her shoulders.

Frederick's voice continues to shift into a lower register. "Let me guess, my sweet girl: he told you he was the baby in the alleyway that night," he says. Her attention perks up. As her eyebrows raise, he smirks. "Have you thought about the notion that he may be a liar?" he asks.

The thought has crossed her mind before, and it causes her to peer off into the distance to ponder momentarily. His grimace grows. "There is a reason he has silenced you from using your tongue. If I were you, I would wonder if I were the chosen one and not him," he says.

She looks back at him. "I suppose that is an interesting thought," she says.

Hearing her agreement sends exhilaration through his body.

His spurt of excitement causes her to question his intentions. "What is in this scenario for you?" she asks.

He scrunches up his face to show his carefree attitude toward the situation. "I just want to support the one whom the shadow has chosen." She nods. Immediately, he extends his hand toward her, and his smile masks his deceptive nature. "What do you say? Do we have an agreement?"

As she peers at his open palm, footsteps sound outside the hallway. Every corpse hiding in the room's dark corners steps forward to stare at the door, and in unison, they hiss at the heavy footsteps, which are growing more robust outside. The familiarity of the weighty strides causes Louise's expression to turn to stone. Her teeth clench to whisper, "Grandmother."

Frederick peers at the doorway with a grin. "If you join us, you will never have to worry about scattering your trivial pieces of cake another day," he says.

Louise's eyes remain fixated on the clamor outside in the hall.

The footsteps abruptly stop, and the heavy, lumbering sounds are replaced by snuffling as the being's nostrils flare, snorting to smell the cake. Its extended tongue unravels to the length of a snake to lick the residual crumbs of the offering.

Louise watches with horror as the driver points the candle's flame towards the wooden barrier, and she notices the being's slug-like tongue emerging from under the door frame to lick up a stray crumb. Her heart pounds faster in her chest, and her breathing stops.

"Together, we can be unstoppable," Frederick says.

The door handle rattles as the tongue retracts like a finger from a flame.

All the noise causes Louise to jump. The shadow figures whisper in a dialect she doesn't understand. While chanting, they drift toward the jiggling handle. As their voices build, the shaking of the handle stops.

Frederick intently stares Louise in the eyes and extends his hand further for her to shake on the deal.

Something in her gut tells her to make the pact, and, remaining locked in a stone-cold glare, she grabs his palm. She smirks as she tightly clutches his grip, knowing she will deceive the old man in the end.

Suddenly, she cannot move. Her thoughts become jumbled as everything outside the driver's gaze blurs. She feels emotionally transported through time, and the connection of their grip causes her to vividly remember every horror that transpired over the past few days. It's as if she were there, seeing the carnage firsthand and dragging the bodies down the stairs to their freshly dug graves.

While reliving the experience through his connection, the echo of his snickering laughter snaps her back to reality. His repulsive raspy cackle ends as his face begins a transformation into something distorted. Bit by bit, his nose becomes infinitesimal, diminishing to an inverted dot that spins counterclockwise like a violent whirlpool, pulling every facial feature that once surrounded his nostrils into the spiraling vortex. As the rotation of his skin swirls faster, all his once-recognizable features, aside from his eyes, blur past recognition.

Unable to move her neck, Louise is forced to focus solely on the centers of his pupils while frozen in a state of shock.

Suddenly, the swirling stops and both eyes close, then immediately spring back open, revealing the color of his once-white irises as impossibly darker than black. Two thick bone fragments sprout through the top of his skull, and blood drips from each blunt-force protrusion. His mouth gains shape with his teeth and lips and forms into an open gape that releases a happy moan. Without warning, each tooth falls from his gums, tumbling to the floor, just like the portrait in the hallway.

Unable to peer down, Louise hears the *tink, tink, tink* of enamel chunks hitting the wooden floor, echoing through the room with the sound of a small hailstorm. The clatter brings her back to the stormy night when their grandmother claimed the vessel that birthed them.

The sides of Frederick's lips twist at each corner to produce a gum-filled grin. As his tongue bounces to the roof of his mouth, pencil-shaped teeth break through the smooth gum line. Within a blink of an eye, his mouth resembles the grandmother's unmistakable razor-sharp smile. His cheekbones quickly protrude, tightening the skin like a drum and creating lofty peaks on his face.

Nothing of his blended appearance is recognizable as human.

Even though she wants to run, Louise feels entranced by the handshake and the ceaseless grip. As the being's appearance nears the end of its hellish shift, she feels the skin touching hers turn scorching hot. She attempts to wiggle her grip away, but with each pull, the grasp tightens.

The transformation completes, and the creature's nostrils flare to sniff the scent of her burning skin. His voice booms so loudly that it rattles the floorboards underneath her feet. "Remarkable. We have a deal," he says.

Immediately, her gaze unlocks from his, and her paralysis subsides. Her voice trembles with fear, as she can now get a thorough look at every detail of his horrific metamorphosis. "Who... who are you?" she asks.

Rain trickles on the roof to signify the rise of a brewing storm. "You don't recognize me, my dear child?" the being asks. He snickers while reveling at the sight of her face locked in a stunned gawp. "I am Frederick. The driver."

Louise breaks free from his grip and, not wanting to play his game, swiftly backs away until her scampering body encounters something still. Immediately, her palms raise to feel behind her.

Frederick's left hand, still holding the candle, lowers it to provide illumination for her curious eyes. "Don't you see? You can't run; we are one now," he says.

Finding a solid grip on a bed frame's mattress, Louise drags herself up and off her shaking legs. "That wasn't our deal. Our deal was an alliance, not ownership," she says.

Taking great delight in watching her struggle, Frederick extends the candlelight towards the hand previously locked in his clutch. Without words, he nudges his chin toward it, motioning for her to survey the tiny appendage's appearance.

Reluctantly, she moves her hand toward the light and notices a piece of skin in the center of her palm that doesn't match the rest.

Frederick lifts his hand and flattens it to reveal the palm involved in the handshake, which has a porcelain-colored patch. "As you can see, we have a piece of one another," he says. He closes his eyes, and his body quakes as he lightly touches the youthful scrap of skin with his tongue. "It's fresh as a newborn babe," he says with a salivating purr. "You can't escape. From this moment forward, you are indebted to me, and for the obligation, I will provide support to make your life a bit easier."

Louise frantically tries to pick off the leathery, callused patch on her hand, but it doesn't budge. She becomes so focused on its removal that she ignores the scurrying and rustling of the mattress behind her, thinking it is only a mouse.

Only after something lightly bumps her back does she turn to look and encounter a set of blue toes attached to an upright day-old corpse. Darkened blood stains the sheets underneath the discolored digits and the body dressed in a house servant's daily uniform.

Immediately, she recognizes the woman's withered frame and gasps. "Ms. Tiller?" she asks.

Gurgling noises sound from the lingering body.

As she watches the weight shift between the maid's two feet, Louise notices clumps of damp dirt lodged between her toes. She stumbles over her words. "I-I thought they buried you," she says.

Frederick laughs profoundly behind her. "I did," he says. "Just because someone is deceased doesn't mean they cannot visit the ones they cherish."

The small girl's eyes drift from the maid's mangled body to her missing head. In shock, her pupils dart back to the blood-soaked sheets. She quickly spins to face Frederick and points her hand at the stagnant corpse. "Bloody hell, there wasn't an ounce of like between us. I am confident she hated us," she says.

Snapping out of its staked position, the corpse's dirt-coated hand seizes the unsuspecting child's pointing finger.

As he watches Louise's frantically struggling limb, Frederick's smile deepens. "The word can mean various things, girl," he says. "Cherish, in her case, could mean obsessed with wanting you to share in the same pain she endured." He shrugs at her attempt to wiggle free.

Unable to unshackle herself from the deadly grip, the child glares at the man and grits her teeth, pouting. "Make her stop!"

"If you insist. But, before I do, you must comply," Frederick says as he lifts the candle back to illuminate his face.

Louise squeezes the lids of her eyes tightly shut. "Yes, fine, I will," she says. She feels the maid's grip release from her finger.

A deep cackle rumbles the room, and in unison, the air turns frigid, and the flame of every candle extinguishes. As Louise wraps her arms tightly around her body, she opens her eyes, and they are met with pitch-black darkness.

The man is gone, along with all the residual chaos.

Realizing she is alone, her heart races as she blindly flees for the exit in the darkness. After some trial-and-error, she enters the hallway. As she carefully shuts the door behind her, she peers toward David's room and notices a sliver of light from a nearby candle sconce illuminating a small pile of leftover cake crumbs. The sight lifts an underlying burden, and a giant exhalation of oxygen exits her lungs. Worry regarding her delayed return and potential tardiness raising suspicion crosses her mind.

A single floorboard lightly creaks. The sound causes her shoulders to shrug to her ears. She has already been through hell, so she wants whatever is about to occur to get over quickly. Her body turns to face all that approaches, and the unsuspected proximity of an individual makes her jump.

Edgar stands a mere fist's width in front of her and stares at her dead center in her pupils. His lips purse with a suspecting scowl. Unable to contain his irritation, he demonstrates his dwindling patience by tapping his foot against the carpet runner on the ground.

Louise's mouth opens with a gasp, and Edgar's presence causes sweat residue to build on her palms. She wipes both hands against her dress hastily to remove the apparent guilt.

He doesn't say a word. Her eyes glance at his tapping foot as she clears her throat. A painful smile twitches on her lips to address his dominant stance. "Oh, my dear brother, you frightened me," she says. His composure remains stone-cold.

Panicked that he may know of her conversation, her communication speeds up as she devises a convincing excuse. "I was putting out the offerings, as you instructed, and I took a small peek in that horrid maid's room to see if any evidence remained from her dismemberment," she says.

Her reasoning breaks his stern composure, and he glances at the deceased maid's room door. "And... what did you discover?" he asks.

With a minor collapse of her voice, she quietly mutters, "It was rather uneventful, I'm afraid. The mess no longer exists, and the room is clean as a whistle. Not even a single drop of blood remains."

The anticlimactic answer causes Edgar's curiosity to shift to anger, and he crosses his arms. "I find your frivolous investigation severely disappointing, considering your brief detour could have meant the end of me," he says.

Thinking he is wise to the details of the complicit conversation, Louise shifts her posture into a rocking motion to calm her pattering heart. Her voice softens to give a short answer. "Oh?" she asks.

He nods as his right hand darts behind him to point at the floor. "You realize grandmother already collected her offerings, don't you?" he asks. Before she can respond, his emotions dramatically ramp up, and he continues. "You are lucky you left an offering in front of our shared bedroom door before the others. Otherwise, I would have been dead. Sister, with your complacency, I would have thought you wanted to kill me." He chuckles at the thought. After giving his laughter a moment to set in her ears, he abruptly cuts the uproar and silently scowls at her.

Her smile grows larger to compensate for her nerves, and her hands play with her dress's material. "If I wanted to kill you, I wouldn't have left a piece of cake outside our door, and I would have hidden," she says.

Edgar raises his hand to his chin to think. "Hmm, I suppose you have a point," he says. At lightning speed, he shifts his aggressive approach. "Very well, then let us get back to our room to get a good night's rest." He extends his hand forward as a peace offering.

Without hesitation, Louise takes it, and they walk back toward the room. As they make their way down the hallway, everything resonates like a horrible nightmare to her, and she attempts to block the memory of what happened in the maid's quarters from her mind.

The small boy opens the door to their private quarters and points to the entrance, directing her to go first. Desperate to end the day and go to bed, she darts into the room, and her body freezes, stock-still in the doorway, upon seeing a man hanging items inside the bedroom closet.

Her brother quickly makes his way past her to ascertain the reason for her pause, and the sight of the driver hanging a new wardrobe for Louise in the closet makes him chuckle at her reaction. "Don't be so silly. It is just ol' Frederick finally delivering you a change of clothes," he says.

As the driver hangs the last article of clothing, he slowly turns to the children. His presence causes the guilt-ridden memory of her disloyalty to return. "Well, isn't this a wonderful surprise, Edgar," she tentatively says.

Immediately, the tiny boy grins at the seasoned man. "Took you long enough. Her wardrobe should have arrived days ago," he says.

Frederick speeds across the room toward the exit, and though he refuses to acknowledge Edgar, he takes a moment to make eye contact with the girl as he passes. The sound of the door shutting breaks the boy's narcissistic bewilderment, and he turns to his sister. "What was that about?" he asks.

She silently shrugs. "How should I know? We both know he is odd," she says.

Her words provide adequate validation, and he nods. "I suppose you are right," he says as he rushes across the room. His hand skims the newly hung wardrobe, and he shouts over his shoulder, "Do you know what this means?"

Louise gulps, and even though she knows what he is about to say, she pretends otherwise. "I daresay I do not know," she says.

His body slowly turns to face her. "This means we can rid ourselves of David sooner than expected. He is no longer of any use to us," he says with a glimmer in his eye.

Refraining from making eye contact with him, Louise hides her panic and rushes to her bed. "What makes you say that?" she asks as she lifts the covers to crawl under.

"Have you forgotten our conversation? Our only purpose for keeping him around was to wait for your new set of clothing, and well, here it is," he says.

Fully clothed, she climbs into bed. "That was our agreement," she says.

He cuts her off to interject his excitement. "So, it's settled. We kill him tomorrow!" Before she can answer, he darts across the room to his bed and hops underneath the feather-filled duvet. With a yawn, his eyes close. "Brilliant idea, wearing your clothing to bed, dear sister. It will save precious time not having to dress in the morning. I fear our day tomorrow will be busy and packed with thrilling events, and we will not have a moment to waste."

His unsuspecting personality leaves her relieved, and she shuts her eyes. "Good night, brother," she says.

"Good night, sister," he says as his voice trails off, falling asleep.

As the children drift into peaceful rest, they miss the sound of heavy footsteps leaving the other side of their door and traveling down the hall. Frederick had been eavesdropping on their conversation, and, quite satisfied with the turn of events, he assuredly makes his way through the corridors' darkness.

In unison, the small girl's lips form a calculating sneer.

Chapter 8

THE TABLE HAS TURNED

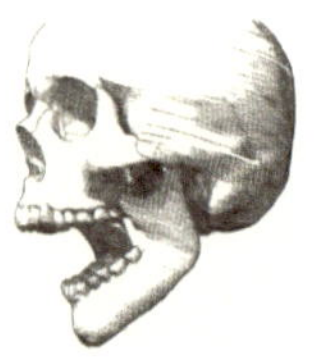

A lone rooster awakens at the crack of dawn. Upon the third crow, rays of fresh sunlight land on the children's faces as they lie sound asleep in bed, and the door to their room swings open.

The noise of the dramatic entrance stirs Edgar awake. Before he can take his first yawn, he feels a firm grasp take hold of his shoulders. His eyelids spring open in a state of confusion, and the sight of both David and Frederick greets his newly awoken stare.

Although clothed in fresh attire, the chaotic state of their hair and their gaping, bloodshot eyes make them look as though they haven't slept in days.

Louise hears the struggle and cracks her lids to tiny slits to evaluate the situation. Not wanting to be involved in the escalating crisis, she remains sedentary and pretends to be sleeping.

As her brother gains cognition of what is occurring, he panics. "Let go of me!" he shouts. His limbs flail, trying to fight them off, but his strength is no match for the two men.

A single punch lands on his uncle's rib, and he huffs out a massive exhalation. The greater the struggle, the more irritated his uncle gets. "Stop it, you ungrateful little brat!" he shouts.

The driver tightens his grip on the upper half of the child's body. Having no luck escaping, the little boy opens his mouth and takes a large breath to scream.

Before the shrill sound can shatter the early morning atmosphere, David fumbles for a hankie wedged in his front lapel pocket. Without an ounce of hesitation, he shoves the piece of cloth into the child's mouth.

Even though a clump of material muffles his voice, Edgar attempts to call for help. "Louise!" he says through the cloth.

The men yank him from underneath the covers and try to stand him up on his wiggling limbs. Pretending he has legs of gelatin, he forces them to lift and carry the entirety of his wriggling body weight out the exit.

As the door slams behind them, Louise cracks her lids a bit more to ensure the room is clear, and, seeing no signs of life, she opens them completely. She slowly stretches her arms out of the covers, and a smirk rolls across her lips. The notion of not having to deal with her brother's discontent makes her the happiest she has ever been. Simultaneously, to her delight, the grown men continue to drag her brother down the hall to the top of the stairs.

He attempts to scream, and his tongue ejects the rag gagging him. "Tell me where you are taking me!" he demands.

His uncle puffs his chest as he prepares to release a much-anticipated dig. Reveling in the moment, he tilts his chin to the ceiling and sucks a long smell of the hallway through his nose. "Well, child, today is the glorious day you go off to boarding school," he says.

Edgar grunts, and his face turns red with anger. "You can't take me yet! I demand you provide me with adequate time to pack my belongings! I am not scheduled to leave for several more days," he says.

The men tighten their grips to constrain his struggle and quickly usher him down the stairs. David laughs. "As you can see, I have changed my mind, and do not fret about your clothes. They will generously provide you a new wardrobe to wear," he says.

The mere thought of his impeccably tailored clothing stolen from him causes the child's eyes to bulge. "Stop this at once!" he shouts.

Knowing they only have a short time to endure the boy's behavior makes ignoring him the rest of the way down the staircase effortless for the grown men.

An older gentleman wearing an all-black suit with matching vinyl gloves and a trench coat waits stoically by the front door. His gray hair grows whiter the closer it gets to his fuzzy sideburns. Both eyebrows tuft together like an owl's furrowed feathers, and the uneven stubble on his cheeks masks the gaunt, sleep-deprived, darkened circles below his spectacles. All of his features are pointed, and their sharpness stresses his age. His growing impatience causes his thin lips to purse tightly as he stands near the exit like the grim reaper waiting for a new soul to usher to the underworld.

The sight of him causes the small boy's eyes to widen. His demeanor becomes frantic as the hair on his arms stands on end. "Bloody Hell," he says, thrashing about. His uncle ignores him, and the driver takes joy in the boy's reaction.

In a last valiant attempt to escape, Edgar gives his arms another few pulls and fails. "What type of boarding school are you sending me off to, anyway? Is that man even qualified? In making your selection, did you consider my high standards?" he asks.

It is evident by the man's calm demeanor that he is not at all concerned with the boy's theatrics. He sneers at

Edgar's struggle. In anticipation of his arrival, his slender hands slowly open the massive entryway door. The rising sun provides a backlight to emphasize the curvature of his scoliosis-plagued spine. "Hello there, child," he says, wiggling his fingers. His deep voice resonates like a tightened bass drum.

Edgar grunts to show his disapproval. Thinking the boy is disrespectful, his uncle shifts his grip to a single hand as he greets the waiting attendant with a quick handshake. "Good morning to you, sir," he says. After finishing his greeting, he loudly takes in a large breath of the morning air entering through the open door and, with a snicker, shields his eyes from the infiltrating sun.

The ghastly arch of the man's back causes a shiver to roll down the boy's spine. All tactics have failed in altering his predicament, and Edgar knows he is running out of time and must immediately devise a fresh approach if he wants to stay.

A new string of manipulative words falls from his lips at a rapid pace. "What about my sister?" he asks. "She was still sleeping. I didn't even get to say goodbye. Honestly, I can't fathom how heartbroken she will be when she wakes to find that you snatched me from my slumber, and she missed my departure." His lips pout to add a touch of validity to his emotional presentation.

Having heard the boy's manipulative tricks before, David coldly responds, "I'm sure she will sleep peacefully, with or without you." The driver fights back a chuckle from his throat and masks the residual noise with a fictitious cough.

As the hacking echoes through the room's large marble dome ceiling, Edgar's head snaps around to glare at the culprit behind the annoyance. He stares daggers at him while giving the man a moment to regain his composure. "Oh, dear, did you swallow a fly? Or better yet, a dagger?" he asks with a scowl.

Unbothered by his lashing out, Frederick clears his throat and ignores him. Even though he has verbally made his points of contention obvious, Edgar's small eyes roll, adding to his expression of displeasure.

The sinewy figure standing beneath the ornate entrance archway finds a sick enjoyment in the boy's torment. Having owned the school for quite some time, he has seen it all and is accustomed to dealing with children deemed bad seeds. As they finish their approach to him, he places his hands on top of his kneecaps to provide stability as he lowers himself to the child's level. The worn joints in his knees prevent him from squatting entirely to the floor. Regardless, he compensates by taking a deeper bend at his waist.

Edgar locks his glare on the man and remains silent. Shifting his gaze to make deliberate eye contact, the man lowers his spectacles. "Young man, let me introduce myself. My name is Mr. Bitterscape. From this moment forward, you will be under my care and shall do what I say," he says.

Trying to contain his urge to talk back, the small boy forces his face to remain stone-cold. His reaction causes the schoolmaster to give a condescending sneer. Shrugging at the lack of verbal response, he pushes back his spectacles and straightens his posture. "Very well, then. Let us carry on."

He glances at the two grown men holding the child's limbs. "Bring him to the carriage," he commands.

They look at each other and nod in unison. Forcefully dragging the little boy with them, they exit, following behind the man as he goes outside.

The sun's rays blind the young child, and in reaction, he squints to protect his corneas. As he attempts to shield himself from the elements impeding his vision without using his hands, he feels a sneeze coming on. Each nostril wiggles and flares wide to stop the annoying occurrence. Though the action circumvents the sneeze, the expanded openings create a perfect entry point for a wafting breeze smelling of fresh horse shit. The foul stench causes his burning nasal passages to force his eyes to peel open.

The sight of the approaching child distresses the black stallion harnessed to the front of the carriage, causing it to paw at the cobblestone, toss its head, and release a chain of loud whinnies. Something about him doesn't sit right with the typically gentle beast.

Behind its attempting bucks sits an all-black carriage with steel accents. Scratches through the paint scheme reveal the mechanical bones, and tiny hand prints taint the carriages only window.

The design of the transportation gives the child an eerie feeling. Given no time to put on shoes, he plants his naked feet into the packed dirt between the pavers on the ground. The wind picks up, creating a miniature tornado of dust that swirls around his ankles. As the men forcefully pull him harder towards his destiny, the skin on his big toes slightly peels from the friction. As they get closer, he notices frilled dark black curtains in the smudged window. "You can't make me go," he says.

Making haste, the schoolmaster jingles a silver metal loop on his pants to find the key to unlock the carriage's door. As his hand stops searching, his arm extends to the sky, holding a severely worn brass skeleton key. With a devious smirk, he mutters, "There you are, my friend." In a diving motion like a jousting match, his fingers thrust the key into the lock, and the sound of the clicking metal brings him joy.

As the man pries open the door, the boy analyzes the interior. Even though the carriage's exterior appears slightly worn, it still comes across as relatively standard compared to other carriage designs; the unassuming exterior shields the interior's far-from-commonplace features, which significantly contradict the outer facade. An ominous secret is hidden behind the lacey details of the rich black-satin curtains: Many metal rods block the door's single glass window, like prison bars installed to keep whoever is transported trapped inside, like a caged animal, the cabin is stripped of all standard comforts, including the traditional bench seat and wall-to-wall upholstery. In their place is stained off-white padding covering the floors and surrounding walls.

Mr. Bitterscape leisurely turns to the men restraining the boy and silently grins. Using his head, he performs a slight jarring nod towards the door, signaling them to put the boy inside.

Without hesitation, a burst of resentment over the child's atrocious behavior emerges within the two men. Seizing the opportunity to enact a bit of revenge, they convert it into a wave of force, and with one giant swing, they throw the boy into the prison-like coach.

As Edgar sits stunned on the floor, reorienting himself from the harsh impact, he notices the door closing, and frantically crawls toward the vanishing sliver of light to escape. Before he can reach freedom, the two men sarcastically wave goodbye, and the door slams closed in his face.

Overcome with rage, he pounds his fists against the padded floor. "Bollocks!" he yells. Trying to make as much noise as possible, he lies on his back, kicking the walls with his feet while screaming at the top of his lungs. "You will regret this!"

From outside, the schoolmaster chuckles proudly as he uses the key to lock Edgar inside. Finished, he safely secures it to the metal ring hanging from his pants and turns to face the men. "Well, gentlemen, your work here is done. Edgar is now in my capable hands, and I assure you that the next time you see him, he shall be quite well-behaved. A new boy," he says.

They are delighted over the realization that the child will be gone. "Excellent," David says.

As the older man nods, he makes his way to the front of the carriage and hops into the driver's seat. While gathering the horse's reins, he notices the boy's uncle rushing in his direction. "Yes?" he asks.

David sheepishly lifts his finger to get clarification. "I am quite embarrassed at not having inquired sooner, but how long will he be gone?" he asks.

The man momentarily stares into the distance to ponder his reply, and a devious smirk forms on his lips. With a slight shrug, he answers, "That depends."

Troubled by Mr. Bitterscape's vague response, David paces as he dwells on the exorbitant monthly fee charged by the man and the ambiguous timeline.

Seeing the man's apprehension, the carriage driver restructures his words to make the small fortune spent on removing the child seem worth it. He chuckles calmly to improve the situation's shifting energy. "I fear you mistook my words. I meant to say that it depends on how long he takes to behave. To ease the disappointment, I'm not eager to give these troubled children deadlines for their treatment. It tends to create an unrealistic hope for everyone. Now, I can tell you that it will not be a simple task. I am certain it will take a profuse amount of time to obtain his compliance," he says.

David's eyebrow lifts. "When you reference 'a profuse amount of time...' Are we discussing a few weeks, months, or longer?" he asks.

Having dealt with many wealthy guardians who wanted to rid themselves of the obligation of children, well-behaved or not, Mr. Bitterscape considers the underlying motive, responding with an answer he is certain David wants to hear. "I can take him off your hands as long as both you and your pocketbook wish me to," he says with a wink.

The response causes David's hands to elevate in adulation and his lips to curl into a wide smile. "Oh, splendid!" he says. "That is wonderful news—as it relates to his improvement, of course." He quickly turns to address Frederick. "Isn't that spectacular, Frederick?"

The driver smirks. "Absolutely, sir. That is excellent news, indeed."

Immediately, the spindly man tightens his grips around the reins and gives a light tug, signaling the horse to prepare to travel. "If you have finished with your questions, I'd best be on my way. We have a long day ahead and limited daylight," he says.

Still grinning ear to ear like a Cheshire cat, David lifts his hand and gives an exuberant wave. "Cheerio! Safe travels, my good fellow," he says.

With a crack of the whip, the horse champs the bit, and the carriage lunges forward.

As it disappears into the distance, David leans over to Frederick. "I daresay, that was easier than expected," he says.

Frederick grins at the distant carriage. "Indeed," he says.

Feeling accomplished over their success, both men turn around in unison and head back toward the estate. David playfully kicks rocks with a giggle and a skip in his step. "Sure is a beautiful day," he says.

Frederick glances at his boss's whimsical step and mutters under his breath, "There we will be many more to come."

Together, with lifted spirits, they enter the domicile.

Chapter 9

IT'S GOING TO BE A BUMPY RIDE

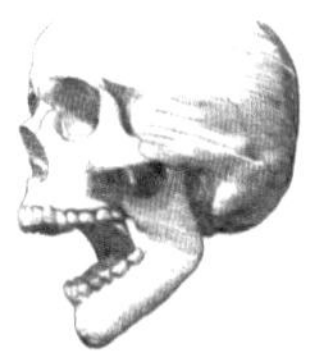

Edgar's tantrum lasts until the carriage reaches the drive's end, and then his focus flips to freeing himself. At first, having no designated seat other than a padded floor seems comfortable for the boy, but the predicament proves challenging over the next few hours. Throughout the ride, he finds every bump causes his body to jump, and each sharp turn uncomfortably tosses him about the carriage like a rubber ball thrown in a four-sided room. The constant jarring coils his intestines into an unwanted knot.

Shifting his travel position, he lies flat on his back and tracks the floor's vibrations. With his eyes closed, he monitors the time between each bump in the road. As he intently focuses on the fluctuating pattern of the carriage's movement, he deciphers when the horse's speed has slowed from a gallop to a trot. Each time he feels the pace of the wheels ease up, he seizes the moment of better stability and crawls on his knees towards the single carriage window. Even though the curtain's material is slightly transparent, the ruffled edges with the closely spaced metal bars and the rocking of the cabin make peeking out the window a more substantial challenge than anticipated.

The idea regarding the plan had appeared foolproof, but like everything in life, it has proved not to be as it seemed.

In the third hour of the journey, Edgar feels the carriage come to a brief halt and darts back to the window. Quickly, he wraps a hand around the mounted bars to maintain his balance in case the carriage makes a start. His opposite hand's fingers snake between the metal bars and poke back a few curtain pleats to peer out.

After being confined to the carriage's dungeon lighting, he finds the mid-day sunlight stings his sensitive corneas, and briefly shies away from the illumination. Taking a deep breath, his head turns back to survey the outside world.

Clouds collect in the sky to obstruct the harsh rays of sunlight, preventing them from being cast over a row of dark-colored brick buildings with dirty, smudged glass windows. As the light dissipates above, a slow-moving heavy fog rolls through the shaded street, and although most of the buildings appear empty and abandoned, waves of heavy smoke rise from a few scattered chimneys. The only form of life on the unwelcoming patch of earth is a malnourished rat scampering through a puddle of brown-tinted water.

As Edgar stares more closely at the stray rodent, he notices the odd reflection of a dark figure in the carriage compartment behind him. His attention shifts to the replica cast upon the glass, and his curiosity over the image quickly takes priority over his thoughts of the rat. Rather than turning around to look, he pulls himself closer to the window to get a better view.

The murky clarity of the image's face makes his heart wildly race. The carriage's interior darkness engulfs a male figure of a sizeable stature. Not having seen anyone else's presence the entire duration of the ride, the small boy feels uneasy and continues to stare at the reflection of the mysterious man.

The unrecognizable entity breaks his dormant position with an abrupt jerking movement. His lurch forward out of the carriage's darkness reveals his dry, cracked lips, gaping sneer, and a mouthful of missing and broken teeth. A crackling scream bellows from his throat and causes the boy's posture to tighten.

Still gripping the metal bars, Edgar slowly turns his upper body toward the man's direction and comes face to face with a view of a partially crushed skull and mangled face. In unison with his movement, the carriage violently picks up speed, and the jolt of momentum causes his grip to slip from the solid iron rod. He tumbles to his hands and knees, freezing in place. Hoping not to have drawn the stranger's attention, he fearfully whispers, "Bloody hell."

The fall attracts the man's attention. Mimicking the child's position, he quietly crawls toward him on his hands and knees, and moves his head closer to his ear upon reaching the boy's still body. Edgar feels a puff of warm breath against his earlobe, and a trickling sensation runs down his spine.

"Boo," the man says.

Immediately, the young boy shuffles back to get away. His back hits the carriage wall, and he helplessly watches with horror as the mangled figure slowly crawls after him.

The turbulent movement of the wheels hitting uneven terrain flutters the ruffled curtain, and a few tiny slivers of light call attention to the man's blood-soaked clothing.

Edgar's eyes dart at the crimson stains, then drift to his gaping jaws. Somehow, miscellaneous pieces of what look to be torn novel pages have become wedged tightly between his broken teeth. "I have a present for you, boy," he says.

Edgar scrambles backward until hitting the wall behind him. He scans side to side, searching for an escape route. "What if I don't fancy gifts?" he asks.

Ignoring the child's snarky remark, the man coughs up a crumpled page with words typed in dark ink and spews it in the boy's direction. He deviously laughs at Edgar's disgusted expression.

Edgar's small leg extends underneath his pajamas to kick away the soggy piece of paper. "Stay back! I am warning you!" he says.

Taking a moment of pause, the man laughs at the boy. Edgar's eyes nervously dart again from side to side. He attempts to buy time by asking questions. "Who are you? What do you want?"

Not hearing a response, he yells louder. "Answer me, you old nincompoop!"

In the corners of the carriage, sounds of repetitive whispers build. "Hope, Hope, Hope," they say.

The sound annoys the child and depletes his patience. He loudly grunts and screams shrilly. "I don't need hope or pity from an old fool!" he says.

Aggressive knocking sounds from the front wall of the carriage, and while continuing to drive, the headmaster shouts, "Silence, my devil child!"

His lack of concern agitates Edgar. "There's a monster in here!" he replies.

The child's remark makes Mr. Bitterscape roar with laughter. "Lying is a sin, my boy," he says. With a crack of the whip and a snap of the reins across the horse's back, he commands it to go faster. "Do not fret; your lying nature is why you have been transferred to my care, and I shall break you of your compulsive habits."

Curious to see the man's response to the knocks, Edgar's eyes tentatively return to the center of the carriage, and the figure is gone. The encounter leaves him confused. He frantically scans the darkness for any sign of the entity's presence, but all that remains is a wadded piece of papyrus at his feet. Entrancing depictions formed by black ink cover the outside of the balled page.

For the next hour of the ride, Edgar crosses his arms and glares at the crumpled piece of paper. The only power he feels he has left over the mocking man is his willingness to stand his ground by refusing to accept the disgusting gift he has left behind. Darkness causes his mind to play tricks on him, and paranoia takes hold as whispers emanate from the corners of the carriage.

The sounds trigger his eyes to peel open and scour for his riding fellow's return. As they become dry from a draft, his white irises become a shade of pink, and bloodshot veins appear.

The whispers continue to build and swirl around him in the cabin. "Take it, take it, take it," they say.

Hearing the command, Edgar rolls his burning eyes. "You have no ownership over me. I am not obligated to listen to you," he says.

A darkened voice overrides the buzz of the chant with a booming command. "Take it!" it says.

The threatening tone causes the boy to gulp nervously. With a condescending approach to show his dominance, he releases a laugh. "Make me," he says.

The carriage's wooden wheels hit a considerable bump upon the last syllable of his challenging statement. It sends the young child violently flying forward, leaving him sprawling across the floor. As he picks himself up, he notices the ball of paper is underneath his chest.

"Take it!" the boastful voice abruptly shouts.

Edgar's complexion turns stark white as his shaking fingers pick up the note. Swiftly, he fights the jarring urge to hurry toward the window to uncrumple the papyrus.

A dark hand emerges from the corner and holds the curtain's ruffle open just enough to provide light for the reading child's eyes.

Edgar's trembling fingers straighten out each paper's crease, and he notices a large image drawn inside. He recognizes the sheet as a page from an atlas, and the image is of a map. It seems too good to be true.

Quickly, he summons the peculiar man who gifted the pertinent item to return, but in the middle of his calls, a loud screech of the wheels silences Edgar. He hears the door unlocking behind him as he sits in confusion over the turn of events. Before he can review the depicted location, he shoves the page inside his mouth to prevent its confiscation and refrains from wincing over the foul taste as the door swings open.

The headmaster towers above him with a psychotic sneer. "Welcome to your new home," he says.

Knowing that if he speaks, they will confiscate the paper, Edgar holds his tongue for the first time in his life while shielding his eyes from the setting sun's glare.

Chapter 10

MAY I HAVE SOME ALONE TIME?

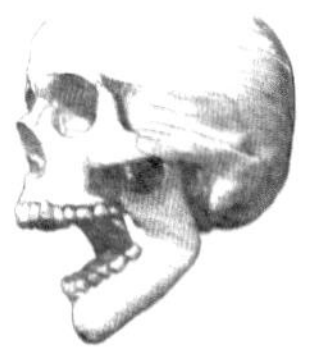

The last bit of daylight blinds the little boy's eyes as two prominent men, who are almost identical in appearance and both dressed in white, hastily approach. Their dark brown oil-slicked hairstyles and facial hair are perfectly manicured, with not a strand out of place.

Before Edgar can glimpse any more details of their features, their hands grab hold of his arms, and he is dragged out of the transportation. When his feet touch the ground, his head darts around to survey the surrounding scenery. Even though the impact shocks his body and makes his heart skip a beat, he clenches his teeth tight to keep the atlas page hidden.

Dead willow trees scatter the dusty weed-infested land, which was once a green lawn leading to the house's front door. The crispy brown leaves travel with the breeze and release an unsettling sound, like pieces of paper crumpled by a clenching fist. Beyond the unkempt trees is an old farmstead. Darkened gray accents the edge of each shingle, drawing attention to its lopsided and dilapidated condition.

As the men forcibly drag him toward his new accommodations, Edgar's eyes frantically survey the paper-covered windows, which block any light from entering the building. The double locks made of steel mounted near the front door handle cause his mind to spiral with dark notions of captivity. *What on earth is this place?* He wonders. Not wanting to face the repercussions of being labeled a problem child on his first day, he regards obedience as his only option.

Each man tightens his grip around Edgar's spindly arms as they get closer to the manor's front porch. Following close behind, the headmaster deviously chuckles, knowing the child's new fate. He whistles a merry tune and ponders how they will teach the boy obedience.

As Edgar's dirty feet reach the porch, the men do not give him the luxury of entering the home of his own accord. Instead, they drag him barbarically behind their relentless march, hitting the fronts of his ankles as they yank him over each wooden step. His eyes squeeze tightly with each painful wince, and his clenched jaw fights not to bellow.

The sound of one man taking a keyring out of his coat pocket causes Edgar's focus to shift to the front door. The front third of a carved gargoyle's head sits mounted to the center of the dark wooden door's paneled surface. Its partially opened mouth forms a condescending smile that frames a tongue made of brass that dangles over its chin. A circular brass knocker ring dangles from its clenched teeth, and its tapping edge rests against the tip of the creature's tongue.

From the corner of his eye, Edgar watches the man insert the key into the first lock. After unlatching it, the man's hand jolts to the brass knocker, and he sounds three wraps against the wood. He then uses the same key to unlock the second lock, and upon its last click, he repeats the knocking pattern. Upon completion of the ritual, everyone patiently waits in silence.

The eccentric process of entering the estate utterly confuses Edgar. To pass the time, he fixates on the head of the gargoyle guarding the entrance while waiting for them to complete the ridiculously lengthy formality. He glares at the brass sculpture directly in each eye's center to search for hidden secrets. While waiting for a cue, he notices the nose of the beast give a slight wiggle. Wondering if anyone else saw the inanimate object move, his eyes dart to the grown men to scan for their reaction.

They, too, remain fixated on the gargoyle and smirk in unison at the movement, as if it is an everyday occurrence. Making eye contact with one another, they give a nod of agreement to proceed.

The man closest to the entrance slowly twists the smooth knob's metal and, once it's unlatched, pushes the door open. As the door creaks to a stop, the men stay oddly still as they look inside.

The longer the boy waits outside, the soggier the piece of paper becomes on his tongue, and the wilting texture makes him want to vomit. Fixated on the irksome feeling, his mind obsesses on the displeasing, starchy consisten-cy, and his face turns a shade of mossy green. Slowly, he senses a bout of oncoming acid reflux, and attempts to free his hands to cover his mouth.

The men restraining him jerk his wrists back to his sides. Luckily for him, the forceful momentum startles him, and without opening his mouth, his throat gulps, causing him to swallow the rising bile. Ignoring the boy's discomfort, the men tug on his arms to get him inside the estate.

There is no light source directly inside the home's en-trance. The open front door provides the only illumina-tion for the dismal space. The layout of the entryway is not the typical design; rather than the ordinary show-case of an ornate wooden staircase leading to the sleeping quarters, the front door leads to a room that resembles an ample coat closet. Solid wooden doors line every wall, each burdened with three locks requiring keys to open.

To an ordinary bystander, the stark design would come across as a makeshift dungeon, not a place to call home. The extensive use of iron deadbolts as a design choice makes it apparent that they are trying to keep something out—or in Edgar's case, to keep something in.

The child's eyes quickly dart to every corner of the dismal chamber to familiarize himself with the room's layout before the door closes and he is left without light.

Without making a sound, Mr. Bitterscape approaches Edgar and lightly pats his shoulder. "You'll get used to it, my child," he says. The boy flinches at the man's touch. The reaction makes him grin, and he retracts his hand. "Or we will force you to get used to it."

Irritated, the child merely wants to get to his room. As if reading his mind, they usher him to a door on the left. The man on the child's right quickly unlocks the door, and they hurry through the opening with him in tow.

Directly inside the room is a narrow, steep staircase that leads to the second floor, and the overpowering men lead Edgar up the steps without a single explanation.

Tiny tears in the paper covering the windows create pinpoint beams of light in the dark stairwell as their feet fumble along the way. Using the light to guide his unfamiliar feet, Edgar's eyes encounter the wooden stairs' rough texture and worn shape. The flexible nature of the porous wood makes the repetitive water damage in the dwelling evident. Each rotting board proves the headmaster's lack of care for the disciplinary school he is running.

Impatient with his slow pace, the men turn Edgar and drag him back-first up the remaining stairs, facing the boy toward the trailing Mr. Bitterscape, who's following close behind them. They briefly make eye contact, and the older man smiles at him, causing a weird feeling to form in the pit of Edgar's stomach.

He turns his head and, looking over his shoulder, discovers they have reached the top step. Another door, this time made of steel, with a padlock, arrogantly stares at them.

The man to Edgar's right leaves one hand gripping his arm while the other fishes out a tiny key from his medical coat. Unlocking this bolted entrance is much faster than the ones before.

Even though the man uses a heavy hand to push the door open, its oppressive weight dictates a sluggish pace.

As the thick metal hinges creak, everyone patiently waits for the gap to widen enough for their bodies to enter.

Becoming impatient with the time it is taking, the man restraining the child's left side squeezes sideways through the narrow space and tugs the boy's arm to follow. The others follow suit. Upon reaching the other side, the boy scans the details of the hidden hallway.

Everything is unmaintained. There is only one way to walk down the hall—to the right. The left leads to a windowless dead-end. The solid wood-paneled walls lining the dim-lit corridor have few characteristics one would classify as decorative. A few paintings speckled with mildew damage unevenly scatter the blank space. Numerous holes plague the ceiling's lathe and plaster above their heads, and dusty white crumbles lay on the floor below each area of damage. A dark burgundy carpet runner adds some character to the worn floorboards, but its inundation with an unknown liquid makes it smell musty and feel spongy to the touch. As Mr. Bitterscape walks ahead of the group, the flooring beneath his boots makes a sloshing sound.

The boy surveys each of his movements with skepticism.

The man's bushy gray brows, perching above his spectacles, raise in excitement as his finger points to reference each painting. Every portrait is of a different young boy similar in age to Edgar, and each exhibits an uncanny likeness to him, with dark eyes and hair considered black on the color spectrum, especially in the poor lighting. Each of the boys wears a matching ill-fitting charcoal gray pinstripe dress suit, and none are smiling; their expressions evoke taxidermy.

The excitement in Mr. Bitterscape's eyes reflects his pride regarding the sight of the collection of portraits. "Each of these young men was once just like you," he says. Reminiscing over memories of each boy he has taken under his wing causes his lips to quiver with a grin only suitable for his devilish character.

As he follows where the man's finger points, Edgar notices each set of eyes is open past the point of comfort, with expanded dark pupils that engulf the whites. Immediately, the correlation of the paintings makes his stomach release a gurgling noise. He glances back at the gray-haired man to read his body language. Something about him is not sitting right with the young boy.

Whispers mimicking the sound of agitated snakes ascend from the layers of paint, and each fork-tongued voice resembles that of the small prepubescent boy held captive within the confinements of the frame. The lack of unison between the mutterings creates an environment filled with overwhelming, chaotic confusion.

Because of his constrained arms, Edgar cannot raise his hands to his ears to keep the garbled mismatched sentences from entangling the depths of his brain, and he is forced to listen. Wondering if everyone else's eardrums are suffering from the many articulated cries, he checks to see where the bevy of chaperones' gazes settle, and he notices everyone is admiring the portraits. Their pleasant expressions make it clear to him that they are not privy to the same haunting speech and unrest, causing his thoughts to spin out of control. Anytime a hiss of an "s" sounds, his pupils jump to the portrait of its origin. He neurotically ponders their intentions. *What are they trying to tell me?*

While the young boy feels himself going mad, Mr. Bitterscape scans each of the children's faces with a look of salvation. His nose snorts with memories of each one, and his head shakes as the thoughts fill his mind. "I have so many wonderful stories of our times together that it is challenging to keep them straight," he says with a chuckle. "Without exception, they were all outstanding individuals indeed," he says, peering into one of the depictions' oddly shaped pupils. He continues to grin.

Edgar's ears perk up at the man's use of past-tense jargon when referring to the children's portraits. Between the jumbling nature of adolescent voices and the men's suspicious behavior, he loses patience and cannot take another moment of anticipation. Believing the answer is worth compromising the safety of the hidden paper, he prepares to ask regarding his suspicions. While looking down at the floor to obscure the view of his rosy cheeks, he uses his tongue to stuff the piece of paper into his mouth's deepest crevasse to speak. He clears his phlegm, breaking the men's idle chatter. "Were?" he asks.

A moment of silence arises from the living, but they quickly return to their pointless conversation. The grown men's reactions make him wonder if anyone has heard his question or if, perhaps, they are intentionally choosing to ignore him.

Meanwhile, his words cause the whispering voices to become more distinct. One by one, the young boys depicted in the portraits take turns to share their accounts. With their bony frames dressed in the same outfit, and their matching hair and eye color, each voice's unique tonal quality is all that distinguishes them from one another. As each portrait's resident takes their moment on center stage, the shadow of the applicable figure partially descends from the canvas. It is as though they are trying to escape their agony. The stiff, tightly quilted material flexes, keeping the boys trapped inside as they attempt to exit their captivity.

Feeling disbelief, the boy swiftly blinks to verify he is not imagining what's unfolding, but nothing changes.

The men appear not to notice the commotion and remain conversing.

As each boy in the frames expresses the extent of their agonizing death, they keep their statements vague to conserve time. One child mentions his attempted lobotomy, another of his death by high voltage shock therapy, and the bulk of the rest recount their dosages of mysterious medicinal concoctions they were forced to ingest. After the last former resident relays his account, the hallway falls mute.

Thinking the parade of guests is over, the young child releases his tense posture to take a deep breath to relieve himself of the heavy words. As his gaze scans the hall, he notices a slight wave of movement around the paintings as the hands of each schoolboy turn to cast shadows towards the floor, their fingers elongating toward an empty frame hanging at the end of the dismal corridor. "It's your turn to sleep, sleep, sleep," they chant.

Even though he wants to argue with their statement, Edgar reserves his contempt and quietly watches. The shadowy hands jar in the opposite direction, creeping closer to Mr. Bitterscape's turned back. "Beware of our despicable friend. A wolf in sheep's clothing is a sinner on the run, and in exchange for our trust, we fell victim to his fun," they say.

Edgar releases a small gasp as the tips of their fingers nearly touch Mr. Bitterscape's hunched spine. The headmaster's ears perk up at Edgar's breath, and as he answers the forgotten question, the shadows disappear into thin air. "Oh, yes. Our establishment prides itself on giving our wards the utmost attention, and because of the extensive therapeutics we provide, we only take in one child at a time. I daresay our treatment isn't for the faint of heart, but it is quite successful. My exhaustive list of tests identifies and weeds out the evil spawn of this Devil-filled world. The stay is rather easy—if you are obedient," he says.

His feet swivel beneath him, and his limbs swing in unison as he pivots to face Edgar. Slowly, with dragging steps, he makes his way towards him. "Each has had quite a similar temperament to you." He takes another slinking step forward, and his body towers over the restrained boy. "Will you behave?"

Even though Edgar didn't feel his question was answered honestly, the man's immense presence makes his chest tighten, and he nods to show his compliance.

His obedience causes Mr. Bitterscape to stamp his boots with excitement against the squishy carpet, and his grin lengthens as he snaps his fingers. "Very good, young man," he says. Quickly, he smiles at the men holding Edgar's arms and gives them a nod for instructions. "He's ready. You can take him to his room now." His hands lift to sound three light claps.

His instruction would seem obscure to most, but both men know precisely what his coded response means. The boy winces as their grips tighten around his biceps.

In a flash, the men's momentum causes their white medical coats to flow behind them as they forcefully drag him past the pinched headmaster. Eager to get behind closed doors, the little boy dampens his urge to fight back and willingly complies.

The way they have scattered the portraits makes the hallway appear longer than it is. The optical illusion leads to a single doorway at the corridor's dead-end. Surprisingly, the images help distract from the odd fact of there being only one room. Rather than matching the rest of the wooden walls' rugged aesthetics, they gave the hidden door special care, painting it a shade of navy blue.

The boy can feel the penetrating stare of Mr. Bitterscape behind him, but then suddenly, as one man fumbles to unlock the door, he turns to take one last glance back, and the man is gone.

There is no sign of him anywhere.

Edgar's eyes fill with confusion over his sudden disappearance, especially considering his slow, lumbering pace.

His upper body twitches at the sound of the bolted door unlocking, and he swivels his head to look. Before he can glance through the opening and peek at his new accommodations, the men shove him inside the room.

As he falls to his knees, their rough handling makes him angry. Wanting to show his disapproval, he spins around to glare at his oppressors, but is met with the sight of a slamming door. He scrambles to his feet and, freeing his lips, expels the soggy, crumpled paper from his mouth. His hands feel the exit for a handle to get out. Expecting to feel wood, his fingers are surprisingly met with cold, hard steel. The door is flat, and nothing adorns it, not even a doorknob.

Horrified by the discovery, Edgar takes two slow steps back to assess the situation.

A sliding screech sound echoes through the prison. Immediately, he notices a compartment near the top of the door opening. A sliver of light darts into the room from the hallway, followed by a set of eyes peering through the slatted peephole.

The boy takes a step closer and recognizes them as the eyes of the man who clutched his right arm and helped drag him through the building. Wanting to manipulate the situation, he shifts his demeanor to cover up his anger with a hint of naivety. His voice quiets with a fictitious stammer. "Who's there?" he timidly asks.

With no one else around, the man feels empowered. The excitement causes his pupils to become brighter, and an out-of-sight smile forms on his lips. "It is I, Marcus, the man who escorted you to the safety of your cozy room," he says.

Edgar, furious he is stuck in the dark, clenches his fists to fight the anger boiling the blood in his veins. "Thank you, Marcus. That was quite helpful of you to assist me with such luxurious accommodations," he says. His teeth clench as he continues. "Whatever did I do to deserve to be in your presence yet again?"

Without taking a moment of pause, Marcus confidently says, "I'm tasked with conveying the rules you must abide by during your stay."

Little melodies sound from the room's corners behind Edgar and soothe his ears. His entire body clenches as he fights the urge to rebel.

Marcus spews the list of regulations like a machine. "There is an outfit on the bed for you to change into. If you don't fancy it, don't complain, we honestly do not care whether you favor the selection. You shall get up at dawn for breakfast every morning, no ifs, ands, or buts; if the sun rises, so shall you. Each night, you will retire to your room by the time the sun sets and keep your sleeping quarters tidy.

Regarding communication, you may write to members of your bloodline, but that is all. As for treatment, you will go through different means of therapy, some harsher than others, to eliminate whatever little devil lives in your seemingly cunning noggin. Remember, we are not your friends. We are strictly here to aid you in your journey to becoming your true self, which requires your pure obedience. Do not talk out of turn, challenge our ideals, or try to escape, because there will be consequences," he says.

Halfway through the list, Edgar tunes out his rambling words with the relaxing tune of the melody being hummed around him.

Marcus squints his eyes to stare at the new patient. "Before I shut you in for the night, I am required to ask if you have questions," he says.

Snapping out of his distraction, Edgar takes a deep breath to formulate a question, but as he forms his first word, the small window shuts, and the crashing sound of metal echoes against the walls of his room.

Chapter 11

JUST AS I LIKE IT, DARK

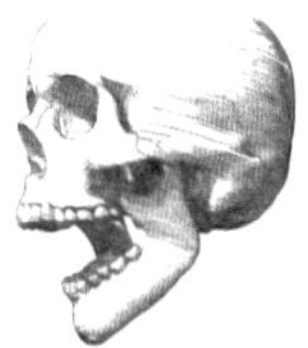

"How rude," Edgar says. His body swivels to assess the paltry room, and his eyes squint to make out the shapes of furniture in the darkness. "Barbarians! They didn't even have the courtesy to provide me a light." As he fumbles through the room, he hears paper crumpling under his bare foot and reaches down to retrieve it.

Voices echo louder from the chamber's corners, and as they meet in unison in the center, they spiral like a trapped tornado. Unable to see his surroundings, Edgar's ears' sensitivity heightens, and his eardrums ache from the straining overload. At the peak of his tolerance, he feels three quick taps against his shoulder blade.

Startled, he turns to see who's seeking his attention. Even though his sight cannot penetrate the murky darkness, he can sense the warm breath of a tall figure. An enormous man with broad shoulders and immensely defined muscles stands still, veiled by the lightless chamber.

The space is darker than a sealed tomb. Edgar has been oblivious to his surroundings, unable to make out his hand in front of his face. He is staring directly at the towering figure standing right before him.

The clueless nature of the small boy fumbling in the dark causes a sick sense of joy to form in the figure, and the adrenaline causes its top lip to lift leisurely, creating a half-smile. One by one, the pure-white coloring of his perfectly straight teeth provides a differentiating hue that subtly stands apart from the shadow-filled abyss.

Edgar glimpses a slight sparkle from the corner of his eye, and curiously, he slowly moves his gaze up to analyze the conflicting visual. As he takes a shallow step closer, he collides with what feels like a giant, hollow drum, and his body bounces off the buoyant structure. Immediately, an off-putting gurgling sound comes from the air above his head, and as he glances up to look in the noise's direction, a thickly built masculine hand lunges in front of his face. Gripped between its callus-encrusted fingers reside a match and a candle with a flameless wick.

A deep voice sounds as Edgar fixates on the offering. "Take it, take it, take it," it says. The words' gravelly texture sounds like a purring cat.

Unsure the offering is legitimate, Edgar's hand tentatively extends toward the floating candle to touch the wax. The sensation of the smooth shell gives him a glimmer of hope, and, becoming impatient, he snatches the items from the air. His fingers compulsively shake with excitement at his discovery and in anticipation of the glow. With the candle stick tightly clenched in his left hand, he carefully sets the crumpled piece of paper next to him and uses his right hand to strike the match against the hardwood floor near his feet. The figure stands still to remain inconspicuous while silently watching over him.

Edgar crouches as he relentlessly attempts to light the match. As the boy's fingers strike it against the floor's rough grain, a sizzle sounds from the top of the small wooden stick, and a flame eats away at the thin, twig-like wood. Worried about losing his only light source, he holds his breath and refrains from blinking as he uses the flickering glow to light the fresh wick. The heat from the newly lit candle softens the top of the taper, causing beads of hot wax to drip down his hand slowly. He plays with the warm substance between two fingers.

While he remains preoccupied, the growing illumination radiates onto the floor in front of him, highlighting a pair of scuffed boots with each flicker. As the light grows brighter, it accents crimson blood droplets upon the roughed-up surface.

Edgar's distraction continues until his eyes glimpse the bloody, worn leather out of his peripherals. The sight reluctantly ends his fun, and he rolls his eyes. "Bloody Hell, why can't everyone just leave me alone?" he says with a huff. His irritation over the consecutive interruptions disrupting his peace causes his fists to tighten around the base of the candle, almost snapping it in two. Taking a moment to break his gaze with the shoe, he acknowledges the shadowy corners of the room. "Can't you provide me with assistance without using these buffoons?"

The foot loudly stomps, and the heel of the boot causes a wave of vibrations in the wood. Edgar's head quickly shifts to glare at the noisy foot, and his face turns a shade of rouge as he hushes the shoe. "Are you dimwitted?" he asks with a rapid, whispering tone. "You are going to draw unwarranted attention to us." More gurgling sounds echo from above.

Slowly, Edgar shifts his pupils to get a better look at the man's face submerged in the darkness. Still unable to see his features, he snatches the crumpled atlas page from the floor and, leading the way with the candle's light, stands. As he straightens his knees beneath him, the unpleasant gurgling becomes louder in his ears.

The man doesn't say a word. Following the movement of the standing child, his head tilts, and an extensive trail of saliva drips from his mouth.

At the same time, the boy loses patience with the delayed reveal of the mysterious man's identity, thrusting the flickering flame in the stagnant body's direction. The lighting glistens against the dripping stream of sticky saliva, and he quickly retracts the candle to keep the slobbering from putting it out. As he moves the wax cylinder through the air, his eyes encounter the man's mangled face. "Dear God!" he says. Intrigued, he moves the flame in a different direction to illuminate his features better.

A quick scan of the tall man's bulky, muscular frame shows that it leads to a sizable vascular neck. Its veins bulge through the pale, bluish skin of the neck's large circumference and support his severely mangled head. His lower jawline is missing, jaggedly removed underneath his severed tongue. Since he physically cannot smile, his amber-toned eyes are the only thing left to show a glimmer of enjoyment, allowing the gurgling noise to be understood as an attempt at laughter. Although he has a distorted face, his cocoa hair remains perfectly styled with a swoop. His top line of teeth is sparkly white, and the surrounding darkness of old blood further shows their perfection.

Whispers taunt Edgar about the encounter. "Hope, Hope, Hope," they say. The words appear to strike a nerve in the grown man, and each of his giant fists eagerly tightens. As his knuckles crack, the sound of gurgling becomes louder.

Unable to focus on the chaos, the boy glares daggers at the shadow behind him. "Who is he?" he asks.

"Hope, Hope, Hope," the shadow chants. The words continue to strike a nerve within the gigantic figure.

As the unsavory noise escalates, Edgar thrusts a hand in the air to motion for him to be silent while he continues to talk to the shadow. "As I told you before, I do not need your pity," he says.

He turns toward the giant and catches sight of his furrowed brow. "As for you," he says as he takes a confident step forward, "you are unwelcome here, so I will ask politely, only once, for you to go." Seeing no sign of movement, he becomes impatient. He furiously waves his hands and shouts. "Leave, now!"

The motionless being stomps his heavy boot like an angered Clydesdale. Before his foot finishes its movement, Edgar squints to glare directly into his pupils. "I dare you to try that one more time," he says.

As they stare deeply into one another's eyes, something shifts in the small boy's compassionless pupils, and they become a shade darker than the room's previously lightless interior. With the abrupt change, his human qualities exit from his being.

Challenging the child's threat, the giant lifts his boot again. Without visually acknowledging his rising appendage, Edgar's voice deepens, and with a mature, commanding tone, he says through his clenched teeth, "Don't you dare."

Defiant of the command, the man continues without concern about the boy's order. Like clockwork, as his heavy step hits the flimsy floor, the sliding window at the top of the door thrusts open. The piercing sound of clanking metal causes them to shift their gaze to the set of eyes peering inside.

Still in a state of hostility, the little boy's voice remains at a low rumble and unrecognizable. Overcome by anger for all he has experienced, he talks slowly to control his spiraling temper. "What do you want now?" he asks.

A condescending voice speaks, matching the one who listed the house rules earlier. It is Marcus. "I did not give you permission to talk out of turn, young man!" he says.

Edgar rolls his eyes and laughs. The blatant disregard for Marcus's authority triggers his annoyance. "Do you find your stay here entertaining?" he asks.

The boy glances at the towering man's dismembered face and then at the shadow. "Which part, sir?" he asks.

His snarky remark causes Marcus's temper to rise, and noticing the candle's flickering flame sets him over the edge. "Where did you get that from?" he asks with a scowl.

The young child shrugs. "I found it," he says.

Overwhelmed by the boy's disobedience, Marcus lets out a deep sigh of disbelief as his eyes disappear from the slat opening and the small door closes.

A demonic laugh resonates from Edgar's throat while sharing his opinion with his unusual companions. "I'm impressed. He is the only person with an ounce of common sense I have met."

The jangle of keys and click of the bedroom locks shorten his moment of laughter. Edgar's pupils dart toward the clamor's location. "I retract my statement," he says as he playfully nudges the gurgling corpse.

The door sluggishly opens with a creak of its hinges, and Marcus enters in a rush. Wearing the same outfit as earlier, he bolts across the room toward the child. His oncoming presence fuels Edgar's dark soul, which lies in wait within his beating heart's confines. Without concern, hand hell-bent on implementing the boy's punishment, Marcus allows the door to shut behind him.

The boy patiently stands, candle in hand, waiting for the headmaster's minion to approach. The thought of being physically battered at his hands makes his blood boil with hatred. The child points the flame in his direction. "I see you, too, have joined the party," he says.

Ignoring him, Marcus continues his angered footsteps in the flame's direction. "I will take that," he says as his hand reaches for the candle.

Already expecting his move, Edgar jerks the candle away, and the flames flicker, causing a reflection of hell to dance in his corneas. His dark pupils slowly take over the whites of his eyes like an oil spill plaguing a body of water, and a twisted grin warps his tiny lips. The orange warmth of the candle's luminosity depicts his adolescent features as pointed and harsh.

Fixed on the child's disrespectful behavior, Marcus takes a bouncing lunge forward to seize the flame again and catches a direct eyeline of the boy's soulless pupils upon his missed grab. His tongue freezes, and his skin turn the color of a newly bleached bed sheet. Marcus's once-aggressive demeanor becomes trepidation as panic takes over his confidence, turning his ego to mush. "No, no, no," he says as his foot takes a massive step backward.

Warmth fills the boy as he absorbs every ounce of energy leaving the adult man's body. Edgar's nostrils flare as he calmly inhales the victory.

Marcus's elbows snap in place and lock straight to his sides. As he continues back towards the door, his mouth attempts to speak, but only makes stammering sounds. "You... you... can't be," he says. Fear paralyzes his emotions.

With the candle in hand, the child slowly approaches the trembling man. His pupils complete the takeover of his eyes as his chin tilts to the floor, and his voice gains a tinge of reverberation. "Say it," he demands with a smirk.

Terrified for his life, Marcus fumbles to open the closed door and realizes a handle does not exist. His entrapment forces him to face the illuminated figure of the approaching demented child. He panics. "I'm sure we can both be mature about this situation. I was only performing the tasks required of me by the headmaster," he says.

The child's face slowly distorts, and his mouth opens. His head cocks to the right, then left, as his throat releases a demonic roar.

Without a choice, the grown man loses control of his actions, and his neck violently jerks to the left to mirror the boy, releasing a sound far from a common crack. His body falls heavily to the floor, the snap immediately turning his limbs to gelatin as a tingling numbness takes over his frame. He attempts to stand, but his legs won't budge; he is like a sitting duck waiting for the approach of a ravenous lion. His breath becomes heavy through the crushed vertebra in his neck, and he lies limply. He is hopeless.

In unison with the tiny child's advance, the jawless man disappears into the shadows that still engulf the edge of the room. Edgar laughs at the man's anguish and the fear dwelling behind his glazed gawping. His voice continues to become lower pitch, and his mouth creates juddering movements. "I know what you did to those boys. You killed them," he says.

"Kill, kill, kill," the shadow heckles.

The sound of the voices chanting in unison fills Edgar with contentment. "And for those atrocities, you must pay," he says.

A dread-derived tear streams from Marcus's eye as Edgar's proper form, hidden beneath his skin, reveals itself. Each of his joints contorts as his external shell sheds to expose the beast that dwells within. His limbs extend, and his body grows tall. His hair sprouts into a polished quaff style, and his body morphs into that of a twenty-year-old man. As he lowers the candle, a well-tailored suit with tails made from the finest black velvet reveals itself, clinging perfectly to his body. He is the spitting image of his father, Daniel.

With Marcus having lost his ability to speak and the functionality to move, the only way to read his panic is through the frantic darting motion of his eyes and the spouting waterworks that slowly trickle down his cheeks. Still, that isn't enough for the boy. After receiving confirmation of the three men's involvement in the horrific acts directly from the children's forked tongues, he demands suffering for their participation in the ghastly torture.

The man shuts his eyes as the transformed child's body takes another step closer. As he observes Marcus trying to hide behind his lids to make a mental escape, a sour taste floods Edgar's mouth. His body rotates toward the used matchstick he left behind on the floor. He shuffles the crumpled paper into his suit jacket, and his hand elongates like a spindly spider's leg to snatch the thin piece of burnt wood. "No! You shall remain present to witness your fate!" he shouts.

Marcus's pinched tight lids spring open at the sound of the shouting. Before the man can figure out what is unfolding, Edgar uses a single hand to snap the match in two, and his fast fingers wedge the jagged pieces to prop open the man's eyelids. "I want to observe the life leave your eyes," he says.

Marcus attempts to blink, trying to quench his drying pupils, but the jagged edges of the splintered wood only further pierce his fragile tissue. Blood drips from the inner corners of his tear ducts, creating crimson trails that run parallel to his streams of tears.

Edgar extends a single finger to wipe a droplet of bodily fluid from Marcus's cheek and, swirling it into the salty excretions, sucks the savory juice from his finger. "Mm... You taste of peaches, my friend. I dare say you perfectly combine savory and sweet," he says. Holding his finger underneath the man's nose, he watches as his parched eyes uncomfortably shift upon catching a whiff of iron. Before a reaction can arise, Edgar lightly traces the contour of both lips of Marcus's sagging jawline and chuckles at the sound of his labored breath.

Familiar whispers echo from the hallway. The sound causes Edgar to fall silent, and, using the candle to illuminate his face, he raises his finger to his lips to signal for Marcus to remain quiet, then uses the silent darkness as a conduit for the schoolboys' voices. As they infiltrate the room from underneath the door, he takes a deep breath to inhale their agony. The taste of their pain fills him with intent, and the impending reckoning brings a smile to his face. Their voices quietly play through his throat and into the tortured man's ears as his slack jaw hinges open.

The cries of past suffering build louder. Every wailing child's voice brings the dying adult more misery, forcing him to acknowledge the horrible violence caused at his hands. Wanting to escape, he attempts to close his eyes again, and the edges of the splintered pieces of wood pierce his delicate skin clean-through.

Upon completing the children's tragic testimony, Edgar whispers in the man's ear. "Those who bring agony to a child shall pay the consequence for their malevolent actions," he says. Marcus tries to scream, but the paralysis prevents him from gathering a deep breath.

Edgar's hand jolts for his open mouth. With a pursed expression, his tongue lightly sticks out from his lips in a state of concentration. Aggressively, he burrows a path through Marcus's esophagus with his fist while excitedly observing his throat's destruction as it crackles, pushing past its elasticity's capacity. Edgar's fist continues its trek to Marcus's chest cavity, and, upon retrieving his still-beating heart, a glorious smile manifests on his face. As he pulls it from the man's mouth, his head lifelessly drops to the left.

Already forgetting he exists, Edgar holds the warm organ up to the candle's flickering light to admire it. "I am all-powerful; I am Edgar. All shall fear my name and atone for their acts of brutality," he says. The smell of coagulating iron causes a ravenous hunger to burn deep in the pit of his stomach. Dangling the organ over the candle, he uses the flame to sear the outer flesh.

In the deep, shadowed corners of the room, a voice chants with a whisper. "Eat, eat, eat," it says.

The organ meat puts Edgar's mind into a state of entrancement as he brings it towards his soft lips. Unable to take the anticipation, he takes a ravenous bite. Blood from the dangling arteries trickles down his chin as he masticates each morsel. He slowly finishes edge to edge and licks his fingers clean of the residual gore.

As the foreign object settles in his stomach, a strange feeling overtakes the skin below his navel, almost as if something scratched him. Curious, he lifts the bottom of his shirt and lowers the candle's light to illuminate the concern. He finds the area's surface red, with a new small tally mark etched into his skin, and knows it signals the first kill committed solely at his hands. With newfound pride, his shoulders elevate, and he drops the shirt's fabric to cover his marking. Shifting his candle away from the corpse, he moves to the small twin bed in the room's corner. The flicker of the flame reveals a familiar gray pinstriped suit displayed over the footboard. Recognizing it as the same one from the boy's portraits, Edgar sniggers. "They should know by now that my taste is far too rich for those rags," he says as he climbs under the single sheet of the bed. Disgusted by the sight of the clothing, he uses his long legs to kick the suit to the floor.

Edgar senses the eyes of the deceased children watching him from the room's corner. Feeling a sense of comfort, he blows out the candle and conceals it with the atlas page under his pillow. As he drifts into a state of slumber, he finds solitude in the sound of deserving mouths devouring the corpse's flesh. "Eat up, little ones. You need your strength, for tomorrow shall be a big day," he says.

A subtle grin remains on his face while his thoughts flutter in a peaceful dream state.

Chapter 12

OH GOODIE, MORE OLD WHITE MEN

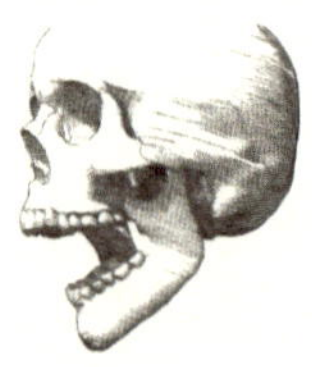

The sun rises outside the windowless confinement, timed perfectly with the sound of a dysfunctional rooster's crows echoing between the four walls of Edgar's room. Having been groomed to awaken in response to a similar morning noise at the Manley estate, his eyes flutter open as his body tosses underneath the single sheet. Unaware of chickens in residence on the boarding house property, the sound momentarily confuses him regarding his current location. "Edgar, remember that you are not at home. You are in a hell house where, if roosters existed, it would only be due to their forced captivity," he says. He continues with a slight chuckle. "I am certain they would live every moment fearing Mr. Bitterscape having a whim to pluck every feather and toe before roasting them alive."

In response to his sarcastic remark, the noise grows obnoxiously louder.

Edgar feels a weight shift on the mattress at the foot of the bed as if someone is adjusting their seat to move closer. The movement causes his adolescent body to roll towards the divot. As he ignores the odd experience, the taunting calls from the ghostly bird escalate in volume and become sharper in tone. Shifting his position, he indignantly wraps the pillow around his ears to mute the noise. The mattress moves again, and this time, instead of ignoring it, he allows a single eyelid to lift and peek.

Perched at the end of the bed is an older man wearing a velvet-piped tailored suit with satin trim around the cuffs and a high-quality top hat perfectly placed on his head. He has a dwindling lit candle in his hand, which provides a warm spotlight on his wrinkled skin. His lips' blue discoloration appears chilly to the touch, and his overall cadaverous hue leaves no doubt he is lifeless. Unaware of Edgar's partially open eye, he waits for the boy to wake, and, becoming impatient, he opens his mouth to create a noise mimicking a rooster's call.

As the sound echoes in the insulated room, it irritates Edgar, and his jaw clenches. He once found the natural call of a rooster calming in the morning, but when executed poorly by an older man, he feels the luster of the peaceful ambiance lost. Trying to escape the torment plaguing his ears, his body tosses and turns as his hands use the pillow to muffle the sound.

The movement of new energy catches the unwanted visitor's attention, and his cock-a-doodle-doo falls silent. He glances to the floor and uses the tip of his polished shoe to nudge the pinstriped suit sprawled across the worn wooden planking. His lips draw into a smirk. "How drab," he says with a chuckle.

Immediately, Edgar's eyes peel open and scan to see what he is referencing, then drift to the man's face. His pupils analyze each wrinkle to determine his age like one would count a tree trunk's rings.

Noticing he has caught Edgar's attention, the man continues rambling, attempting to form a camaraderie with the child. "Such a shame," he says. His throat clears as he pauses and glances swiftly to ensure Edgar is still listening. "My guardian tried to send me to a place like this when I was about your age. It ended up being quite a pivotal moment in my life."

The boy lifts his head from his pillow to get a clearer view. "Oh?" he asks. Making eye contact with the visitor, he inquires further. "What did you do about it?"

His questions perk up the tufts of hair in the lean man's ears. He has experienced nothing similar; he lived a very privileged life in which his parents put him on a pedestal and rewarded his bratty behavior. There was only one time when he was powerless and did not get his way, and it occurred during his last moments on earth.

As he attempts to muster up a story depicting a believable account to tell the child, he briefly looks away, and a devious grin builds. The ends of his lips curl whimsically as they pull apart to sprout an enormous smile.

As the boy waits for a response, he shifts his cover to his hips and props himself against the headboard. The shadows in the room mock him with whispers. "Hope, hope, hope," it says.

Irritated by the interruption of their conversation, the child lets out an angry grunt and grits his teeth. "For the last time, you dimwits, I do not need your charity. For once, someone with clear life experience is trying to help, and I demand you not ruin it," he says.

The man finds the child's silencing command to be most entertaining. "Well said, my dear boy," he says. The man puts aside his resentment over the specifics of his demise, especially the fact that it was at a woman's hands, and, thinking on his feet, he playfully flips the conversation's direction. "Please let me introduce myself; my name is Harold, and regarding your fine question... have you heard of the poisonous qualities of poppy seeds?"

His answer sounds like a fun discussion to the child's ears. Wanting him to continue, he gives a vague answer to prompt him. "Yes, to an extent. As I am sure you are aware, I am well read concerning most literary topics," he says with a slight smirk.

The man grins at the boy's answer. "Based on your intellect, you sound as if you could have been one of my children," he says. Noticing the child's attention waning, he clears his throat to get the conversation back on track. His wrinkled hand reaches into his lapel pocket and pulls out a small cream-colored handkerchief with eyelet lace around the corners. As he extends his hand with the gift, his smile twists in a way the child did not think humanly possible.

Feeling unsure over the man's eerily changing demeanor, Edgar glances at his creased hands, then at his shifting lips.

While the man is waiting for the boy to take the offering, the hesitancy makes him impatient. "If you do not want to accept my gift, it is quite all right. To be honest, I would rather keep them for myself," he says. As he retracts his hand, he slightly turns his body to hide his peeking eye.

The gesture causes the boy's glance to become frantic. "Wait," he says as he lunges across the bed to snatch the folded handkerchief from his hand. "It's rude to offer a gift and take it back."

Getting exactly what he wants, the man fights back a chuckle. "Indeed," he says.

In the corners of the room, whispers sound from the shadows. "Hope, Hope, Hope."

Each taunting word pierces the aged man's eardrums and causes his grin to diminish. His anger builds as his eyes begrudgingly dart toward the taunting, but just when he is at his wit's end and about to speak, the young boy has an outburst, causing him to fall silent.

Before speaking, the child opens his mouth and grunts to show his irritation. Dramatically rolling his eyes, his fist hits the mattress. "Bloody hell, enough of that nonsense. This is the last time I shall tell you. If pity is all you are to offer, leave my life forever, or I will seal your mouth shut myself," he says.

His harsh words cause a twinkle in the man's pupils.

As silence falls over the room, Edgar carefully unwraps the handkerchief to see what's inside. Tucked in the center of the cotton fabric is a large clump of prematurely harvested poppy seeds.

Having high expectations that the gift would be monetary, Edgar doesn't hide his disappointment and glares at the man with a bitter expression on his face. "You have got to be kidding. What am I to do with these? Do you expect me to farm a harvest locked in this prison?" he asks.

Irritated by the child's snarky remark, Harold leans forward in silence with a stern glare, and his building anger finally causes him to snap. "Listen, you ungrateful little twat, it took a significant time commitment to harvest each of those tiny poisonous candies. If you don't show at least a tinge of gratitude toward my efforts, I will single-handedly shove each of those tiny presents down your dry throat and joyfully watch the life leave your eyes," he says.

As he finishes his outburst, like the flip of a switch, he recovers from his tirade, smiles, and returns his body to its original relaxed position. "You shall know when to use them."

Without breaking eye contact with Harold, the small boy carefully coils the ends of his cloth back up to cover the seeds. From the corner of his eye, he notices movement in the shadows behind the man.

A well-dressed figure, similar in appearance, but half his junior, emerges from the corner. As he approaches, the heels of his freshly polished boots clink against the floorboards, and his palm lightly rests on the older man's shoulder. They look like twins from different generations.

Having had no time to himself, the child finds the extra company annoying, and he hopes they will both leave. He speaks at the speed of light to conduct a haphazard introduction. "I suppose, based on his friendly gesture, you two know one another," he says.

Harold glances at the man next to him with a smirk. "Indeed. This is my son, Robert," he says. Both men share a snicker.

Edgar finds their happiness annoying and their presence a nuisance. "Oh, joy," the small boy says. Not wanting to continue the conversation, he changes the subject. "Dear sirs, I hate to be the bearer of bad news and upset this quaint two-person family reunion, but I fear my new caregivers will arrive within the hour to wake me for the hell they have in store. They will not favor you being here; like me, you will have no choice but to face their wrath if you do not go. You both should get on your way and leave me in peace," he says.

As they open their mouths to reply, he cuts them off with a condescending smile. "Good day, and Godspeed."

Instead of being met with fear of Mr. Bitterscape's wrath, the son's chuckle turns into a full-on cackle. The noise makes the boy cringe. "Would you like me to scream? They will be here in minutes if they hear my shrieking call," he says.

Robert's laughter grows louder, and a tear from his hysteria escapes the blue-tinged corner of his eye. He gallops across the room near the door and points to the mangled body on the floor. While passing by his father, the candle's flickering flame highlights his purple lips and ghostly white skin. "Will I face a demise like this gentleman over here?" he asks. Slowly, he squats and clicks his tongue against the roof of his mouth.

Immediately, the boy's gaze locks on the man playing with the corpse, and he rolls his eyes. "He must have slipped during his nightly check," Edgar replies. Swiftly, his pupils shift to keep tabs on the older man, but he is gone. The end of the bed is empty. The man has vanished, and all that remains in his place is the carefully wrapped offering and a fading chuckle.

The son continues to probe the limp corpse. "We can continue with that storyline if you wish. Honestly, I think your work is quite impressive," he says.

Wanting him to leave, Edgar raises the volume of his voice. "Shouldn't you go? I am certain your father is missing your company," he says.

Without looking back, Robert grins. "Oh, we are not close," he replies. "You say this man slipped? Well, if that is your story, I, too, must confess. The two men you hope to save you from my company, Mr. Bitterscape, and his minion, will not be joining us. Because of unfortunate circumstances, I must disclose that they have choked on their morning cereal."

Edgar's eyes squint to analyze if Robert is telling the truth. "How do you know?" he asks.

The man's smile grows wider as he recollects witnessing every horrific moment surrounding their long, agonizing deaths, and he casually shrugs. "I just do," he says as he reaches inside the dead body's pocket for the keys. Standing, he brushes off his trousers and snakes his arm through the door's window slat to unlock the outside. As the exit swings open, he continues. "You have little time if you are to make it back to your rightful home before dinner is served."

Still skeptical, the child inquires further. "Why are you helping me?" he asks.

"Don't you mean, why are we all helping you? Let's just say that there is some unfinished business that needs to be tended to," he says.

Edgar looks down at the handkerchief and scans his blood-stained pajamas. He wonders why no one has provided him with a fresh change of clothing among all his gifts. "If you are such a wise man, how do you suppose I shall be suitable for dinner in these tainted rags?" he asks.

The man has vanished. All that remains is a dead body surrounded by a glossy pool of scarlet red and the whispers stemming from the room's shadows. "Go, go, go. Flee, flee, flee," they chant.

Edgar spots the opened door and glimpses Marcus's set of keys in the pile of gore. He smirks. Without a second thought, he springs from under the covers and leaps to the floor. As fast as he can, he grabs all his random trinkets from underneath his pillow and places them under his arm. Not wanting to lose his opportunity, he rushes for the door, snatching the keys as he passes by the burgundy liquid. As he exits the confines of his room, he notices something peculiar about a once-empty portrait frame hanging in the hall.

It now depicts the three men who once ran the school in a close-up portrait standing side by side. Their eyes match those of the children—pure black pupils dilated into the whites of their eyes. Child-like giggles echo from the confines of the other frames as if welcoming the re-cent additions. In unison with their joy, blood seeps from the bottom of the corridor walls, sloshing as it rapidly covers the floor. "Go now!" the children shriek.

Knowing there is no time to waste, Edgar tightens his clutching arms around the items tucked away under his elbow and sprints down the staircase of the rickety home as each painting of the children soaks the hallway in a river of red fluid, making every likeness unrecognizable.

His exit's beginning seems like a blur. As he fumbles for each key to unlock the steel doors, his mind fixates on the need for a swift escape. Reaching the last lock, he notices scarlet smears down the walls that he presumes to lead to the kitchen. He looks closer, and the streaks appear equiv-alent in beauty to a work of art. Some are whimsically swirly in design, and others have long straight lines.

His feet take a step back to admire the delicate brush strokes. As he takes a moment to survey the design, he notices that each makes up a well-crafted letter of the alphabet and, when joined together, creates a message. As he is about to read the words aloud, the door thrusts open, startling him.

A small man named Fitz, with an ill-fitting toupee and black fringed crocodile boots dances through the home's front entrance. Edgar notices his bashed skull poking out from underneath his mismatched brown patch of borrowed hair, and his eyes fixate on the man's gruesome appearance with a look of utter confusion. "Who are you?" he asks.

Fitz gives a sizable open-mouth smile to greet Edgar. "It is I, Fitz. Your savior," he says with a dramatic bow.

Feeling the stout little man has ruined his moment of concentration, Edgar ignores him, trying to continue deciphering the bloody massacre's message. Finally, he can make out each cursive letter, and he realizes it creates the word *H. O. P. E.*

"Bloody Hell!" he shouts upon realizing that it is the same useless word that had tormented him throughout the ordeal. He throws a tantrum, storming past the ridiculously dressed man with his ludicrous white ruffled shirt waving in the breeze and stomping out the door.

"That's the spirit!" Fitz says as he follows behind the boy.

Edgar sees an all-black carriage with a single coal-black horse waiting outside and quickens his pace towards it. Hearing the obnoxious man's footsteps following closely behind overwhelms his mind with irrevocable irritation. As he gets closer to the ride, he glances to the front of the carriage at the driver and is not pleased with what he sees.

An enormous powdered white wig sits atop the head of a child-sized man dressed in a gaudy baroque-textured tail coat and matching knickers. He bears a similar child-like stature and head injuries to the toupee-wearing buffoon. As Edgar approaches, he gets a better view of the man holding the reins. He has an identical face to the obnoxious one tailing his pace, and the realization that the two are alike stops him dead in his tracks.

Fitz's mousy toupee flops in the wind with every springing step. In his oblivious state, he doesn't see that Edgar has stopped, and his feet slide, kicking up dirt and rocks as he tries to avoid running into the boy.

Fitz feels important for his minor role in facilitating the child's escape. Franz, his twin brother, enjoys the same excitement, as evidenced by his overzealous waving hello from the driver's seat. "Hop aboard your ride to freedom, young man!" Franz shouts.

Not wanting to be stuck with two dimwitted grown men on a lengthy ride, the child's eyes frantically look around for another escape option. *What is this? Did they send two clowns to transport me to a second-tier circus?*

His eyes pause on the back end of the carriage, and his lids narrow to squint. A black pantleg with a purple calf and scuffed boot protruding from its cuff hangs over the side of the wooden luggage compartment. Edgar stares, bewildered, while attempting to devise a narrative for the odd scene.

Without warning, the leg twitches, causing the dangling boot to fall to the ground, exposing the sockless foot and blackened toes, which wiggle one by one.

As the boy stares in confusion, his head tips to the right to attain a different view, similar to how one would observe a piece of abstract art. Mid-focus, he notices Fitz's mousy brown toupee fluttering in the wind as he rushes to the fallen boot and scoops it from the ground with an annoying laugh. He quickly loosens the worn laces and, struggling with the foot's fighting movements, tries to put the boot back on. "It is almost as if he wishes a draft to bring consumption to him," Fitz says, letting out a string of loud grunts and groans to make all aware of his efforts.

Franz hears the commotion and hops from his seat. The spastic movement causes his curly wig to tumble to the ground. He snatches it up from the dirt as he passes, rushing to assist Fitz. Realizing the wildly flailing foot will take two people to manage, he haphazardly tosses his wig onto his head to free his hands to help. The two men attempt to grab the foot and stuff the shoe back on, but every attempt proves futile.

Stuck in disbelief, the boy watches with amusement as Fitz and Franz battle the unruly appendage.

The two men try a fresh approach, deciding to lift the lid of the heavy wooden trunk and stuff the misbehaving foot back inside. As Franz stands on his tippy toes to shove the top open, several stray curls of his robust hairpiece catch the latch, and as the cover flips open, it steals the powdered pouf from his head.

The infiltrating light creeping into the once-sealed wooden compartment causes the corpse inside to awaken and lift its sleepy head. Edgar catches a glimpse of the corpse's upper body. He notices that the man is wearing a uniform matching that of a traditionally hired driver, which he finds an interesting twist to his devised story-line.

Fitz, distracted by his brother's tantrum over the loss of his wig, is oblivious to what is transpiring in the wide-open trunk. It is no longer just a foot that they must contend with, but the entire corpse, free of its confines, sitting upright in its make-shift coffin. Franz paces as he problem-solves how to reach his wig dangling just out of reach, and Fitz, realizing his brother is of no use, returns his attention to the shoe dilemma and comes face-to-face with the trunk dweller.

Terrified and ridiculous, he lets out a loud squeal while hurling the scuffed boot at the decaying man's head in what he deems self-defense. The heavy sole hits its target, knocking the man back into his containment. Seizing the moment, Fitz reluctantly grabs the dangling leg and shoves it inside the compartment with the rest of the festering body.

His hairless, bumbling partner is oblivious to the scene unfolding under his nose due to his fixation on the breeze dancing across the bare skin of his skull and his insecurities over his shiny topped appearance. Franz is only focused on saving his precious curls, along with his dignity. Without a second thought, he jumps as high as his little legs will allow and bats at the lid, knocking it closed. "Success!" he shouts upon realizing that his prized hair is now within reach.

Unbeknownst to him, Fitz's fingers are nearly squashed by the slamming cover, and he is livid. Swiveling his body, he faces Fransz while furiously stomping his feet to get his attention. "Bloody Hell, you almost cut my precious rings clean off my fingers!" he yells as he holds the gaudy ringed-filled digits up in front of him, surveying for any possible damage.

Franz snickers as he adjusts the curls on top of his head. "What if I were to disclose the act was intentional?" he asks.

Though angered by the lack of concern, Fitz pretends to be unfazed while indignantly adjusting the ruffles of his shirt and dusting off his pants. "Oh, really? And why is that?" he asks. His body language contradicts his words, leaving no mystery over his rising anger.

To torment him further, Franz insults his taste in fashion. "You do realize your ruffles are rather out of style? I, for one, wouldn't be caught dead sporting substandard garments such as those on my delicate porcelain skin," he says.

As their disagreement escalates, Edgar becomes impatient, loudly clearing his throat to get their attention. "Excuse me!" he shouts. Both men are consumed by the petty fight and ignore Edgar as they continue to take low jabs at one another.

No longer entertained by their tomfoolery, Edgar takes fate into his own hands and storms to the side of the carriage. He reaches for the handle and quickly opens the door. As he climbs inside the cabin, he is met by a black velvet suit, polished shoes, a felt-brimmed hat, and a prestigious golden cane displayed across the beautifully upholstered seat.

Whispers from the darkness call to him. "King, king, king," they say. With a devious smirk on his lips, he slams the door shut behind him.

The loud noise startles the men, and they swivel to look for the boy.

Franz's curls bounce while his open hand whacks his brother's shoulder, and he grunts. "See? What did I tell you? There you go again, scaring the child. You must work on your temperament, brother. It can be quite ridiculous sometimes," he says.

Fitz's face turns an angry shade of red while he rubs his arm from the sting of the slap. Remembering he has a mission to complete, he holds the small patch of flopping hair to his head with one hand as he sprints to the carriage. He loudly steadies his breathing to calm himself while reaching with a nervous hand to open the door.

The hinges release a low creak as the entry slowly releases. Edgar rotates to see who is invading his privacy and is angered by the site of a lone eye peering around the door's edge into the dark cabin. "What do you want?" he asks.

Clearing his throat, Fitz opens the door further and notices the boy has changed into the rich velvet black suit with tails. "I see you have found the clothing I left for you," he says. Worried about being scolded, he remains rigid, almost as if he is tiptoeing on eggshells.

Edgar stares straight ahead toward the darkness to contain his underlying fury. "So it appears," he says.

Taking his words as a welcoming gesture, the man attempts to hop inside, but finds himself met by an icy glare and inexplicable force blocking his entry. "What do you think you are doing?" Edgar asks. "Did I invite you to join me?"

Fitz immediately tries to cover his embarrassment with a panic-stricken chuckle. He scurries backward, vehemently apologizing. "Of course, of course! What was I thinking?" he says. He begins to shut the door while glancing back at Edgar one last time in hopes of receiving an invitation.

Something about Edgar's face has shifted, and his expression is unsettling. He almost appears inhuman, silently glaring at Fitz as if preparing to speak. "Yes?" Fitz asks with a nervous gulp.

Without blinking, Edgar looks over the top of his head and lifts his nose in blatant disregard. "Has anyone ever told you that your hair does not match?" he says with a sneer.

Standing outside in an awkward state of hesitancy, Fitz's hands fling to his head, covering the hairpiece, and without saying a word, he quietly shuts the door. He glances at his brother before adjusting his toupee in the reflection of the carriage's polished surface.

Franz signals it is time to go, and Fitz scrambles up next to him in the driver's seat. Knowing there will be a fight over who will steer, they compromise by each taking a single rein. In unison, they sound a crack of leather against the horse's rump, enticing the steed to pull them forward on their journey.

Feeling the momentum of the carriage picking up speed, the boy sits in the cabin's dark solitude, contentedly engulfed in the shadow's presence. As he opens his jacket to place his offering securely inside, he feels a slight prick against his fingertip. Curious, he retrieves the item from his pocket and smiles at the small, splintered piece of bloodstained wood. "Hello, old friend," he says as he carefully places it back in his pocket. Having his mementos close to his heart brings him a sense of peace he has never felt before and puts a permanently etched grimace on his lips.

As he allows the shadow to infiltrate his soul, he feels comforted. His eyes close, and as he reviews the past several days' events, a reassuring whisper fills his ears to help him sleep.

"Sleep peacefully, for you are the king. We will transform thee with our rightful pleas. When you wake, we shall see just how powerful you will be," they sing.

Chapter 13

WHY, HELLO AGAIN

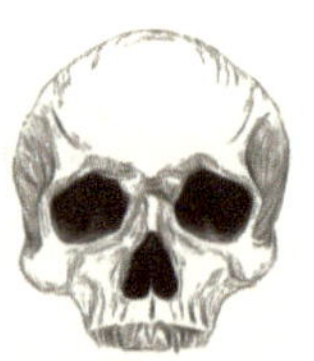

For once in his life, everything seems peachy-keen. As the carriage hits bumps in the road, his mind remains in deep sleep rather than waking. In fact, unlike the long, torturous journey to the boarding school, the trek back to the Manley estate seems relatively short and pleasant. The recurrent crack of the horse's reins signals the commencement of a glorious event and causes very little annoyance to his sleep.

Whispers chant from the darkness surrounding him. "Wake, wake, wake. It is time for you to take your rightful place while the others congregate. You can't be late," they say.

As the carriage slows, the boy yawns and stretches his arms. With a smile, he hurries his body towards the lavish curtain window to peer outside. Night has fallen across the land. A yellow glow from the stars and a partially cloud-covered full moon peeks over the roofline's steep shingles. Inviting candle and fireplace flames reflect off the interior side glass of the large picture window, and a torch provides illumination on the porch. Crickets chirp outside the window.

Immediately, he thinks of the first time he arrived at the manor and the excitement each rich detail brought to his eyes. Seeing the estate now brews an underlying irritation in his gut. The grand entrance no longer appears as significant to him, plaguing his mind with notions of deceit. Tired of reflecting on his feelings, his hand closes the curtain with anger, and the boy throws himself back into the seat.

He chuckles to the shaded bench across from him. "They all shall regret the day they cast me out like trash," he says.

The incompetent male duo claiming to be his chauffeurs struggle in their attempt to open the carriage door, and Edgar becomes impatient. As he glares across the carriage into the profound depth of the shadows, his foot taps the floor to count each passing second. "They are utterly ridiculous. You must have been lazy on the day you chose two grown men with such poor intellect," he says.

After the third tap, he loses all patience and lunges to open the door. "Must I do everything myself?" he asks. His fingers clutch the handle in a mad rush, and he aggressively turns it while glaring at the shadow.

Deep laughter ascends from the interior of the carriage. Each slightly distinct voice intertwines into a small swirling storm within the cabin. As Edgar cracks the exit, he grunts at the mocking room.

What sounds like a light breeze pushes through the small opening and joins the boisterous group's chant. "Hope, Hope, Hope," they say.

One by one, the men who provided Edgar odds and ends throughout his journey manifest beside each other in the coach. In unison, they lift their right hands and playfully wave. Not wanting to waste another moment on the ridiculous gathering, Edgar releases a tremendous sigh and rolls his eyes. "Bumbling fools," he says.

Trying not to engage them, he swings the access open and hops outside. Without looking back, he shuts the door. "They had their chances at life, and shall not ruin mine, nor detract from my glorious entrance."

Stars paint the sky above with twinkles in the darkness. The graceful wind brushes against his cheek, and he smiles. "It's good to be home," he says. Taking in the moment, he closes his eyes to center his mind. "I am all-powerful, and this manor is mine."

A short, muffled shriek cuts through the peaceful ambiance of the familiar setting.

As his lids spring open, his eyes hunt to find the source of the glorious scream, and his gaze is drawn to a flickering candle in a window of the upper story's hallway. "That's strange. I don't remember that end of the manor being occupied," he says.

Before getting too carried away with thoughts over the ominous noise, he starts toward the door. Everything seems livelier than usual. It is almost as if someone has prepared the estate for a guest's arrival. The single torch guiding the pathway to the entrance flickers brighter in tandem with the added jubilance of his quickening steps. With a light chuckle, his feet shift to a galloping dance. "It is a beautiful eve for a toast, and it will be glorious to surprise the host," he says.

Edgar springs up on the stone-inlaid porch. With a triumphant click of his heels, he locks eyes on the inviting knob, and his lips form a smile as the suspense builds on his fingertips.

Unprovoked, the knob preemptively twists. As the door slowly opens, he angrily clenches his fists. *Who dares take the opportunity of surprise from me?* His mind festers as the entrance widens to reveal Frederick.

His presence wipes Edgar's smile clean from his face. "Oh, it's you," he says.

Nothing has changed in the driver's appearance; his eyes remain black and soulless, his body wears the same uniform every time Edgar encounters him, and even the dirt stains remain from the day in the garden maze. The young boy's disdain puts a sadistic grin across his face. "I am glad to see you've returned. We were expecting you," Frederick says as he steps aside to let him in.

Edgar's feet remain frozen in place. He is confused. "You were expecting me?" he asks.

Frederick motions for him to enter. "Now, come inside before you catch a chill."

Edgar blankly stares straight ahead as he enters the ornate, marble-filled foyer. Having dreamt of the day he would make his dramatic entrance and shockingly return, the fact of them preemptively knowing of his arrival irks him. Unable to let go of the notion that someone has informed the household of his impending arrival, he swivels to face the man and slowly scans his dirty clothing as his gaze makes its way to Frederick's soulless pupils.

Frederick returns the stare as his arm reaches behind his back to shut the door. "I am quite certain you are dying for me to answer your question. We received your letter yesterday to inform us of your expected arrival. Though you stated it might not be 'til next week, we prepared just in case and are happy to have you back earlier than expected," he says. With a smug look, he takes a deep breath to continue.

Edgar immediately identifies a few holes in his account and interrupts his explanation. "With only being at the school for a mere night.... how would it be possible to get a letter to you within that short time?" he asks.

Frederick snickers to make light of his skepticism. "You must be suffering confusion from the fatigue caused by your lengthy travel. It has been months, dear boy," he says.

"That is inaccurate. I slept quite well on the ride here and am certain it was only a single day, so you are mistaken," Edgar says. His throat clears to release a condescending huff. "Aren't you curious about how I managed to escape?"

His babbling does not entice Frederick to seek the answer, and he retains a straight face. "It was all listed in the letter you sent, and they released you; there was no talk of escape," he says. As he walks ahead of Edgar, he motions for him to follow.

Planting his feet, the boy refuses. His petite hand extends. "I would like to see this letter you speak of," he demands.

Frederick stops, and with his back facing Edgar, he hides a smirk. "Very well," he says as he rummages through his coat pocket. He pulls out a crumpled piece of paper and tosses it over his shoulder.

Even though he finds the presentation disrespectful, Edgar scrambles to the floor to retrieve it. As he stands, he carefully straightens out the crinkles. Immediately, he analyzes the structure of every letter etched into the discolored piece of papyrus. The letter's dark-burgundy ink smells faintly of iron and does not reflect his meticulous grammar and proper diction. Even his name has suffered misspellings.

Rather than confronting Frederick, he glances at the waiting man's fidgeting hands. Squinting, he notices a reddish stain on his fingertip; knowing the driver's behind the letter, he switches his approach. "Please forgive me. I must apologize. You are quite correct. I remember writing this, and as it says in this detailed account of my stay, I have been away for longer than I recollected," he says as he skips to catch up.

Frederick slowly turns to face him. As the boy looks into his eyes, he passes the letter back with a smile. "Silly me. I must have been having too much fun at that wonderful establishment you sent me off to. What's that saying? 'When having too much fun, one loses track of time?'" he says.

Expecting a confrontation, Frederick reluctantly takes the letter back and shoves it deep into his pocket. "Yes, that must be it," he replies.

Edgar races ahead with a hop in his step. "Now, where are the rest of my wonderful family? Dinner, perhaps?" he asks. Without an answer, the angelic mural silently snickers at him, and he continues towards the sound of clinking plates in the dining room. The driver quickly attempts to catch up.

As he barges inside the dining area, Edgar scans the table and notices three place settings. Immediately, he remembers the last time he stepped foot in the room and misses the essence of the gruesome scene. Looking again at the configuration of the dishware, he finds it odd. They have carefully laid two place settings of ornate porcelain dinnerware at one end of the table and a single place setting at the other.

Why would our dear uncle be sitting so far from us? While contemplating the non-customary table arrangement, footsteps approaching behind him cause him to jump. He turns, and his gaze meets the faces of his uncle and sister. Even though he loathes each of them, he puts on a pleasant façade. "Surprise!" he says. "I know it must be quite shocking." He playfully giggles.

Their mouths drop open with surprise as they stare at him. Feeding off their state of shock, he escalates the pace of his speech to exude a sense of excitement. "I am aware you weren't expecting me until next week, but I was on such great behavior, those wonderful men let me come home for my visit early," he says.

David breaks his silence with an open-mouthed smile and claps for one of the kitchen staff to attend to the room. "Such wonderful news! Much has changed since your leave, including new staffing. I shall have another place set for you immediately," he says as he frantically claps again. While waiting for someone to enter, he looks at the boy and motions to his outfit. "How ironic. I laid out a dress in the same forest-green fabric for your dear sister to wear."

The door leading to the kitchen forcefully opens. Even though he hears the commotion of a table place being set, Edgar leaves his stare. His uncle's reference to his suit's color being green and not black disconcerts him. Biting his tongue, he decides not to battle the opinion. "I must have miscounted. I would have sworn there were already three table settings," he says.

David rushes around him to the opposite end of the table. Rather than following his movement, Edgar shifts his focus to his sister's face, and she attempts to avoid him by looking down at the floor.

The sound of chairs being dragged across the wood causes the boy to turn, and he notices his uncle has pulled out two seats for the children. He pats the cushions to motion for them to take a seat. "There is another thing you missed while away—we have a guest staying with us. I feel you two shall get along. She is lovely, and I am very much smitten," he says.

Glancing at his sister, he sees her fighting back a chuckle and finds similarities in their reactions, almost rekindling their relationship. "Oh?" he asks as he makes his way to the chair.

The children take their place at the table and make themselves comfortable. Taking a seat himself next to them, David looks off into the distance and daydreams about her walking through the door to join them. "Yes. Just wait until you meet her," he says with a sparkle in his eye.

The boy looks to the open doorway with a smirk and nudges Louise's leg underneath the table. "She must be something special," he says.

Immediately, David speaks to answer him. "Indeed," he says.

David nervously falls silent as the sound of a woman's heels approach. With a harsh screech, he slides his chair away from the table to get ready to greet the arriving guest under the golden-arched doorway.

Simultaneously, every sconce mounted on the surrounding walls fizzles out. All that is left for lighting is the dim flicker of a few wax-dripping decorative candles on the wooden dining table fit for a banquet. The warm

lighting reflects off the gold linen decor and the arrange-
ments of decadent fruit centerpieces.

As the woman steps inside the room, David rushes to be
by her side.

A strange voice echoes behind the children in the shadowed corner. "Monster, monster, monster. She's a monster. Kill the monster," they chant.

The children look at one another with a grin. Edgar
leans near his sister to whisper. "This shall be fun," he
says.

While the smitten couple quietly talks, Louise whispers
in her brother's ear. "I'm so glad you are back. They've
been ignoring me ever since you left. I missed you, brother," she says. Knowing they have little time, she swiftly
continues. "What do you suppose we should do?"

"I think I have something that shall do the trick," he
says. Keeping his eye on the couple, he reaches inside his
jacket pocket for the poppy seeds but finds his rummaging fingers met with a shocking discovery: it is empty.
"Bollocks," he says as he frantically checks again.

Louise's eyes nervously dart to him as her uncle and the
mystery woman make their approach. She elbows Edgar
to get his attention, and upon stopping his search, he
stares at the woman with a mischievous smile.

The woman looks confused to see the children sitting
at the opposite end of the table. David helps her into her

seat and rushes back to sit next to them. Surrounded by awkward silence, he nervously clears his throat before introducing the guest. "Dear Hope, this is my ward, Edgar. Edgar, this is the beautiful Hope I have spoken so fondly of," he says.

The boy's body stiffens at the sound of her name. Subtle sounds of chanting echo into his ears. *Hope, Hope, Ho pe.*His thoughts run wild as he realizes the correlation between her name and the shadow's repetitive chants. He finds the circumstance comical. His grin widens, and his chest fills with air as he holds his breath to fight back his laughter. *She was the one they had been trying to tell me about. They were not pitying me... merely trying to warn me of her.*

The child, distracted by his spiraling mind, feels transported. In his swirling state, her words sound like mumbling in his ears. Anytime he needs to appear engaged in the conversation, he nods with a grin or gives a generic response like, "We've heard so much about you." He can't help pondering what she may have done to make the shadow despise her.

Sounds of clapping pierce through the air. Edgar's eyes respond to the harsh noise first, and his mind follows suit. Looking at David, he realizes he is calling for drinks to be poured into their cups for a great toast. The sequence of events reminds him of the last moment he had in the dining room before they sent him off to imprisonment, and he fights the feelings of resentment.

A voice whispers only loud enough for him to hear. "Die, die, die," it says.

The door to the kitchen opens behind them. The butler enters the room in a flurry, glasses in hand, while turning his face away from the dim lighting to prevent exposure to his identity.

Edgar gazes at him with unnatural intensity as he pours the deep red wine into Hope's, then David's chalices. Maintaining his watch on the butler's steps, he sees a small handkerchief drop from the back of his work trousers. As it flutters to the floor near his seat, he realizes it is identical to the one gifted to him by Harold, the old, well-dressed man. Thinking it's an interesting coincidence, his lips purse at the sight of the others raising glasses and ingesting the contents of their cups.

The air in the room grows chilled, and the children look at each other.

David immediately releases wet coughs deep in his esophagus, tumbling forward, hitting his head, and shattering the dinner plate in front of him. Edgar's eyes grow wide with wonder, and he tugs on his sister's dress to get her to look.

As their uncle convulses on the shattered porcelain plates, they hear footsteps approaching from behind, and a hand lightly touches their shoulder.

It is their father, Daniel.

Briefly sharing eye contact, they turn in unison to watch and admire Hope's final suffocating moments. The sound of her head hitting the table comforts the children, and, wanting to see the life leave her eyes, Edgar hops out of his seat, grabs a burning candle, and moves to her side. His father follows in the shadows behind him.

As she loses consciousness, her eyes glimpse their threatening presence, and a single tear falls from her eye as she mourns her death. Within her last moments, everything slows to a calm solitude, and the shadow bids her farewell. "Sleep tight, my child," it says. Her eyes slightly flutter to acknowledge the voice.

The boy immediately realizes she can hear the ominous being. Impressed by her ability, he seeks advice and kneels beside her, meeting the level of her stare. His smile grows sadistically long. The small glimmers of life left in her irises disclose to him the backstory of her life, and he finds her fight to break away from the shadow weak and pathetic. Disregarding her journey, he mocks her with a cackle. "Mors tua, vita mia," he says.

Slowly, the choking sounds in her throat stop, and her eyes become lifeless.

Edgar springs to his feet. "There is no room in this world for the weak," he says as he looks at his sister and brushes off his pants.

Sounds of clapping quietly start from the darkness of the room's corner and grow louder. Edgar lifts his hands to acknowledge them.

The candles on the table simultaneously blow out; the only light that remains is the single flame clutched in his grip. Each sound of clapping hands is joined by chanting voices. "King, king, king," they say.

As he lowers his hands, the orange hue from the small flame illuminates Edgar's face. With every flicker of light, the shadow of their father becomes translucent armor over his flesh. Slowly, their faces become one, and his limbs sprout, causing him to stand taller.

The sight of his morphing appearance makes Louise's pupils dilate in fear. Suddenly, the sound of heavy footsteps catches her attention, and she turns to witness Frederick barging into the room. Terrified about what may happen next and concerned over her own best interests, she opens her mouth to warn him of the events that have transpired.

Edgar's ears burn with her disloyalty, and his head swivels to face in the opposite direction. His voice becomes gravelly in texture and low in pitch.

The scene causes Frederick's feet to plant underneath the dining room's golden-arched entrance as life is sucked from his skin. With a smile, Edgar's feet lift from the floor, and his hand extends toward the man.

In a panic, his sister stands to help. Hearing her movement, Edgar lifts a single finger, and an unseen force immediately pins her back down to the chair. "Sit, you disobedient brat," he says.

He's not the same, and the timbre of his voice terrifies her. As her heart pounds, her eyes dart between her brother and the man who swore to protect her.

As the boy's feet continue to levitate from the floor, his ankles go limp, and his lifting hand causes the grown man's body to lift in unison. With a slight flick of Edgar's wrist, Frederick's head bashes into the golden arch, twisting the vertebrae in his neck, and his body falls heavily to the floor. He can't move; a bone in his neck has shattered, and as he tries to escape, the veins in his eyes bulge from the strenuous effort he exerts.

The girl squeals at the horrible sight of him, paralyzed and defenseless.

Edgar carefully lowers himself to the floor, and his jaw opens with a deep laugh to reveal a serpent tongue. Wanting to see his sister's distress, he slowly looks at her.

Both of her palms shield her eyes from the unfolding sight. He glares at her cowering demeanor. "Your actions just validated my suspicions, Louise," he says as he takes a proud step with his newfound height toward her.

Still hiding her eyes, the sound of his slinking step creates more fear in her bones, and she stutters. "I-I don't know what you are talking about," she says.

Laughter comes from his throat and projects to every corner of the room. "I know everything," he says. His fingers point to the room's edges. "The walls have heard and relayed to me every treacherous word, child."

Moving to stand beside her, he sets the candle back on the table, slowly pries her hands from her eyes, and orders the shadows to restrain them. "I want you to observe what happens to those who disobey me," he says as he reaches into his pocket. With a sickening grin, he retrieves the blood-stained wooden matchsticks and uses the points to prop open her eyes.

She tries to scream, but nothing comes out. As blood trickles down her cheeks from the pierced skin, Edgar uses a finger to wipe a single drop and licks the residue. The taste causes his pupils to widen like a pod of dispersing spiders. "Your voice is no longer useful to me," he says. Reaching into her throat, he extends his fingers and cuts her vocal cords with his nails.

No matter how hard she tries to fight him, she can't win, and drops her head in defeat.

Bored with her new submissive personality, Edgar slinks back to the driver's body to have more fun.

Even though her head tilts to the floor, Louise endures the unfolding scene with the light of a candle and the forced propping open of her eyes.

As he approaches the fallen man, Edgar's smile stretches from ear to ear. While each crease of his lip distorts, his body morphs into a monster so vile that, even though it's lifeless, the legs of the dining table shudder.

Not wanting to look directly at the scene, Louise can tilt her head just enough to view it through shadows, and it horrifies her to find that Edgar's shadowy portrayal is not a young boy, but the grandmother figure who had visited them each night.

Frederick attempts to roll his body, but is met with limpness in his limbs and torso. The creature jerks its knees into a marching procession while staying on the balls of its feet. As it makes its way toward him, it releases a demonic snarl, calling for the shadow to flip the man over.

Granting his wish, the shadow provides a gust of air that boosts Frederick's body to a different position while hideous laughter sounds in his ear. He now has an unrestricted view directly facing Edgar, but unlike the boy's familiar childish features, everything has changed.

The porcelain skin of Edgar's face has shifted into a canvas of tight semi-translucency. His eyes are twice the size as before, with soulless black pits engulfing their lidless confines. Purple veins, bulges, and red, bloody splotches show through the thin layers of skin. The bottom half of his body is primarily composed of a large, low-sitting belly, and his limbs appear too emaciated to match. His feet are oddly tiny for his new stature, but the long, thick, discolored toenails make up for some of the missing feet's length.

Panic floods the driver's eyes, making it clear he regrets Edgar's last request. The unmistakable sight of the ghastly figure causes terror to run through his core. Frederick's mouth gapes open, releasing a blood-curdling scream, and the creature follows suit, opening it to match and mimic the chilling shriek.

As the creature sucks in an enormous breath of air, the man's large body moves, and he cannot use his hands to stop his momentum. The dragging of his heavy frame causes the silver buttons on his pants to create deep scratches on the wooden floorboards.

Continuing to consume the oxygen in the room, the boy's creature-like body lowers its arms to the floor to get on all fours. His slinking limbs now resemble a giant spider. As its elbows unnaturally hinge, its mouth expands into a grimace, pushing the boundary of its jaw into a bone-breaking stretch. Beginning with his feet, the creature's mouth engulfs the driver's body bit by bit. An imprint of bulky boots is visible in his throat as each leisurely gulp progresses Frederick's body down Edgar's esophagus.

The shadows on the floor in front of Louise portray the gruesome scene in dark, monochromatic depictions. Even though her drying pupils are forced to watch the shadow puppet show unfold, her mind is curious about the accuracy of the murky depiction. Unable to take another moment of mystery, she tilts her head to look and catches a horrifying glimpse.

Frederick's head is the last thing remaining outside Edgar's enormous anaconda-like mouth. His glossed-over eyes have the eerie look of a hopeless cry for help.

Edgar lifts his chin to allow the rest of the man's body to slide down his throat into his belly, and as his victim disappears, his stomach expands with an imprint of his outline.

As he casually rubs his belly with his spindly claw-adorned fingers, Edgar licks his lips and helps his unhinged jaw relocate. Chuckling, he turns to face Louise. "Would you like to be my next delightful treat?" he asks. She attempts to shake her head no, but her muscles and tendons will not comply.

The candle's melting wax has dwindled to a stub. As the monster steps closer to the light to better reveal the horror of Edgar's transformation, the shadow cast behind him reflects something completely different—a familiar boyish adolescent body. As the creature stands stagnant in front of her, Edgar's thoughts order his boyish shadow to speak, and it takes on a life of its own. "I am she, and she is me," the boy's shadow version says.

He points next to him, and a darkened grandmother creature manifests with a grin to match his. Louise's pupils dart around with terror, and her eyes widen as the two link hands. He continues. His opposite hand lifts to welcome another being into the shadow-mural on the wall. "And he is me, and I am he," he says.

Following the cue, the outline of Daniel joins their dark auras and links hands with the boy. Together, they stand in an unbreakable chain resembling an unfolded paper-people cutout.

"Together, we are unstoppable. To be quite honest, your support is no longer needed. You have become a rather unnecessary nuisance," Edgar says, smirking and shrugging. The other shadows follow suit, shrugging and smirking in unison.

Whispers sound, swirling and bouncing from the walls of the chilling room. The small boy chuckles as his ears decipher the inaudible speech. "Don't be so cruel; she served a purpose for a tiny stint," he says.

Quickly, he redirects his attention to the girl. "Can you believe it? Our endearing shadow would prefer I kill you." Dropping his counterparts' hands, Edgar's shadow ponders the thought while pacing along the room's walls. "But don't you worry. I clarified that it would be far too easy a punishment."

Her red eyes scan the room in a panic as the wooden splinters dig deeper. With her head turned and her eyes diverted in her shadow brother's direction, the terrifying monster in front of her silently morphs into a slightly older version of the boy's original mold. As his limbs and appearance contort, the thread of his clothing changes to a pure black velvet with decadent matching accessories. His left hand holds a golden cane, and his head supports an expensive top hat. Noticing that she is still fixated in deep contemplation on his youthful shadow puts a smile on his face.

The young boy's shadow suddenly freezes, and he turns to address Louise. "I'm sorry to be the bearer of bad news, but I am afraid you're not real. Well, it is real that only one of us can win, and of course, it is me! Did you honestly believe that your kind, helpful self could overcome my magnificence? You are weak, and I am quite embarrassed to think that because of our close relationship, I could have an ounce of your useless characteristics incorporated into my superior being. So, with that being said..." he says.

Taking a moment to enjoy the sound of her heavily beating heart, he lifts the outline of his finger and points at his favored manifestation, standing next to her.

As she looks at him, Edgar's new frame aggressively strikes the bottom of his cane against the floor three times, as if calling a meeting to order. "I declare I shall tuck you away from this day forward, and no one shall know who you are. It shall be quite refreshing to be subjected no longer to your empathy. It was rather exhausting," he says. As he cackles demonically, the flame of the flickering candle goes out.

Louise is left in the darkness, and her heart races. She hears whistling, then steps running in her direction. As she feels immense pressure against her skull, her vision goes dark.

With a dainty flick of his wrist, Edgar releases a slight bludgeon of the hard stick to knock her out briefly. Continuing with his jolly tune, he drags her limp body out of the dining room, and as he exits, he waves to the flying cherubs above. They giggle at him. "We will await your return. Please come back soon," they say.

Gripping Louise's arm with a single hand, he raises it, gives them a slight wave, and, in unison, waves his own. "I shall! Good day!" he says.

He departs through the waiting exit as whispers echo from the foyer. "King, king, king," they chant.

Taking a moment, he inhales the fresh air as the grand entry doors slam shut behind him. Excited for this new chapter in his life, he takes a second to remember the moment, inhales to smell the surrounding aroma, and howls at the moon. As his head levels to the ground, he thrusts the small girl's body over his shoulder and heads directly to the waiting black carriage.

Seeing the men who once drove him to his destiny still missing doesn't bother him. Instead, he uses his creativity to derive a better solution. He skips to the compartment in the back, remembering the mangled man and his haphazard movements.

A bronze skeleton key waits in the keyhole, and the sight makes him sigh. "Maybe he can be useful," he says as he unlocks the heavy lid, thrusting it open with all his might. The girl feels light as air as he balances her weight over his shoulder.

Using all his strength, he drags the worse-for-wear corpse out of its satin-lined prison. Upon tumbling to the ground, its mouth immediately gapes open, and its lungs gasp, filling with air.

Wanting to have a conversation with the man, Edgar throws Louise into the compartment of the dark trunk and whispers inside, "Good night, dear twin. This shall be your new captivity. Like a caged animal, you will no longer have the desire to sing joyfully or the freedom to frolic."

The man on the ground is still delusional as he reclaims himself.

Edgar's hands reach down to remove the freed man's shoelaces from his boots, and he quickly uses them to tie Louise's limbs together. Brushing the dust from his hands, he slams the lid of the trunk and locks it shut. He removes the key and admires its significant beauty in the moonlight.

Gathering strength, the locked-away man rises to his feet and watches Edgar easily swallow the key. As the metal travels to his stomach, he turns to introduce himself. "Hello there, chap; my name is Edgar Manley. For payment of saving your life, you shall be indebted to me as my chauffeur," he says with a grin.

Speechless, the man nods. He briskly lumbers toward the front of the carriage, losing his laceless shoes on the way. He pauses and opens the side door for Edgar to enter, then moves to the front, takes his rightful place in the driver's seat, and grasps a single rein in each hand. "Where would you like me to take you, sir?" he asks.

Edgar pats his hand over the inside pocket of his coat. Upon feeling a slight bump, he reaches inside and pulls out what he was searching for—the crinkled page of the atlas. He straightens it and, for the first time, studies its contents. The image in the moonlight brings a cynical smirk to his lips. As he gallops to climb inside, he happily shouts, "What have you heard about the United States?"

Still trying to gather his bearings, the driver takes a long pause. Not caring to hear his answer, Edgar doesn't wait for his reply and continues. "I've heard it referenced frequently as the land of the free, and the thought intrigues me."

Hoisting himself into the carriage, he pauses. "According to this page from the atlas, there is a port not too far from here, and that is where we shall go."

He quickly jumps back out and hands the page to the driver. "I assume you can read," he says.

The driver places both reins in his right hand and reaches out with his left to grab the paper. He holds it up to his eyes and scans both sides of the page. They are blank. Not a single mark is on the papyrus. "Sir..." he says.

Confident he will ask for assistance to decipher the map due to his illiteracy, Edgar lifts a hand to silence him. "Never mind; cue the steed. The shadow shall lead you," he says as he pivots to the cabin's opening. Hopping inside, he slams the door shut and, with the curtains pulled, lets the shadow-filled interior engulf him.

As he makes himself comfortable, he smiles at the seat across from him as Daniel appears. "Hello," Daniel says with a mischievous grin.

With a crack of the whip, the wheels of the carriage roll on, full of excitement as they embark on their journey.

Chapter 14

I'M NOT DONE

To my loyal followers,

Please do not concern yourself with the safety aspects regarding my lengthy travels, because I indeed did not. To further ease the insignificant agony, I found every moment following our departure to be both picturesque and pleasurable. I beckon you to remember that stressful thoughts cause aging, which diminishes our desirability. How else do you think I maintain my charming appearance? It is strictly superficial; I don't fret over frivolous topics.

Regardless, I must remember I can be very magnetic, and presumably, you have taken a liking to me after reading the first part of my life's tale. If someone forcefully downgraded me to live through your eyes, I suppose I would also take a liking to me. Your flattery is why I will continue to relay what has happened since I rode into the night.

Let me generously begin with a rhetorical question: Would a celestial being be concerned about death? Yes, you heard me correctly when referencing omnipotence. I am considered relatively superior by humanity's standards. I am not bashful about the matter; in contrast, I am proud.

It is advantageous for and quite astute of you if you gathered following that breathtaking scene in the dining room that the shadow now inhabits the entirety of my being. I must say, the final transition was quite magnificent. My only disappointment is that I wish it would have happened sooner. Breathing the same air and sharing the same thoughts makes me feel alive, and as our hearts beat together, we are unstoppable.

I am the chosen one, and unlike the other fools before me, who allowed their pathetic feelings to abolish their loyalty or let empathy for their victims get in the way, I am unwavering in my devotion. If you are wondering, the shadow has since disclosed the identities of those knick-knack-giving men who aided my journey as Hope's band of ex-betrothed. I must say, they have made for the quite entertaining company throughout my travels. Before I get off-track with idle gossip, you shall be aware that I let the shadow manifest me into a vessel for its power and my devotion, so I am forever protected from harm. The entity made the expectations and compensation very clear the night we merged.

Upon my exodus from the estate, everything surrounding my departure flowed perfectly. Like clockwork, a local maid traveled to my uncle's estate from town to tend to the chicken coops on the edge of the property, and that day was no exception. Her sunrise arrival barely missed the sight of my carriage leaving the tediously long driveway.

She fed the poultry and continued with her usual routine of fetching eggs. That morning, when she knocked on the front door to deliver them to the kitchen staff, she found it was unlocked and opened on her first rap. To her, the open door was nothing other than good fortune. Greed took hold, and she let herself in, hoping to collect a few things to improve her financial position.

She made her way to the kitchen to rid herself of the basket of eggs so her hands would be unencumbered for gathering. She was finding it peculiar and fortunate that no one greeted her arrival. She wandered into the dining room in search of silver candlesticks, and, rather than treasure, her eyes encountered David's corpse, and the sight threw her into a state of shock. As she scanned the room, the view of the other mutilated corpses overcame her and sent her running. She immediately reported the horrific discovery to the local police jurisdiction.

As this was all unfolding, the driver continued doing just as I asked, and completed the tasks with the help of the shadow. The man was not the brightest of flames. While they pointed their condemning fingers toward her, touting her as a sinister witch, the shadow took hold of the reins, and we rode on our merry way.

It was nothing personal against the girl; it was all merely a part of an excellent plan that meant more than her pitiful humanity. She should be thankful that we delivered her from a life of poverty.

The night they hung her, I swear I could feel the pressure of the rope tightening around my jugular, and in unison, the life leaving her body. The sensory experience was indescribable and addictive. It's hard to put into words, but all I knew was that I wanted more. The pureness of the euphoric high, and the rocking sensation of the carriage, sent my mind immediately into a deep slumber, and I was at peace, or so I thought.

When I awoke to the stopping momentum of the ride, the sight of the rotten bones of the wretched school that had held me hostage sparked my quick temper. Taking a moment to breathe, I knew at once that the shadow had brought me here for a bigger plan.

I stared out the small window, and the carriage's wooden wheels must have only been stagnant for mere minutes before we heard another pair of hooves clopping against the rocks of the abandoned road.

Squinting at the approaching intruder, I recognized it as an official postal cart. Following protocol, they searched for my uncle's next of kin, the lone heir to the Manley estate. and delivered the news of his death and the details of my inheritance to the address David had listed for me within his will.

Immediately, I considered my aged appearance and the dead men within the walls of the hellish confinement. With no time to spare, I rushed to the front porch to prevent the people from entering and to preserve the illusion. As soon as they came to a stop, I greeted them, using my maturity to my advantage. I put on the best performance of my life while pretending to be the establishment's owner, and thanks to the school's shady form of operation and lack of relevant records, the task was straightforward. Finding the architecture of the manor's outer appearance creepy, they finished their business quickly, all but throwing the envelope with the inheritance documents order at my feet. It was like taking candy from a defenseless child.

As they sped away, I placed my hand on the house door handle to pretend to let myself in and allowed them a few minutes to fall out of sight. Then, with a smile, I hopped back in the carriage with my fortune, and the driver continued our journey to our last stop. The estate remained in my name, and it gave me added comfort to know I had a place to return to if the need arose.

After collecting a substantial sum from the family cash hoards, I secured a one-way ride on the first ship set to depart to the Americas. If you wonder whether I have misspoken, I have not; I only purchased a single ticket. This is the point in my narrative where I must confess the fate of the man transporting me and squash all your enthusiasm surrounding the idea of a brainless driver standing beside me as some amusing sidekick. Take a seat if you must, for I'm about to dampen your mood.

I knew from the beginning that any man with a mind idiotic enough to get lured into the confines of a trunk would weigh down my journey, and his buoyancy confirmed my philosophy in two ways. While waiting around the dock for ticketing, I ensured no one was looking and shoved him straight into the port's water. Lucky for me, my suspicions were correct. The rhythm of his fully clothed, weighty body's comically flailing limbs attempting to swim could not tread the choppy water. It was good riddance.

So, with that knowledge, you should know that when I use any instance of the word *us*, the verbiage refers to Louise in her trunk prison and me.

Before that moment, I had never been on a boat, but I found the rocking waves quite relaxing. I used the long ride to reflect and draft my plan of action for what my new life would be; I knew I had to get my story straight. Through my internal reflection, I found peace with the shadow taking hold of my heart and whispering in my ear. We kept each other company, and didn't need anyone else.

Upon stepping onto the soil of my new home's land, we implemented the minor details of the plan. Still, I prefer to keep the ornamental information between us, and am only permitted to share with extreme vagueness my story from this point forward.

I began my new life in America, purchasing a new wardrobe and taking up residency in a town called New York. You may be curious about what happened to my dear, sweet sister. Well, not wanting to give too many details, I made a unique home for her within the beautiful brick walls of the building I call home. Louise's confinement hides deep in the back of a closet that I rarely, if ever, disturb. Occasionally, though, I find her silence comforting if I feel an ounce of loneliness, and I will press my ear to the door to hear her faint breaths.

That is enough about her. As I close my letter, I will say that the United States has lived up to its name. It truly is a land of the free. I have found it is a place where you can do almost anything you want, whenever you want, and frankly, I would consider their way of living simply lawless.

So far, during the first part of my residency, the panic surrounding the Great Depression has made finding trusting souls to play with relatively easy, and, mixed with the elements of the cruel winters, if you don't wait until they are frostbitten, they provide an effortless stock of food.

It is interesting to be the piranha in a fishpond filled with guppies. Here, everyone willingly believes I am just a young man who has lived a tragic life riddled with parental abandonment. They all feel charity towards me; the upper society pities me for gaining wealth from orphaned circumstances, and the poor trust me with the hope that I will provide them with money. Unlike where I grew up, I find the culling order of societal ranking like a lively game of cat and mouse. Regarding the gritty details, I am sure you can use your imagination.

While I let you chew on that, there is one more thing I find fascinating here: It baffles me how much they love their newsworthy content, especially stories filled with brutality. I think they prefer it. Unusual disappearances also seem to be a favorite. It doesn't matter how big or small the individual's status is; they will always take notice, and the fear the information causes in the population's eyes brings me comfort. It's almost like the government wants to start a frenzy, and I love every moment.

As I smile, writing my thoughts on this piece of papyrus, I must stop myself before sharing too much. Maybe in this lifetime, we shall meet again, perhaps finally face to face, and if we shall, I beckon you not to be a stranger, for I always love the revolving company.

Just remember, we all come to perish eventually.

To anyone who shall make my acquaintance, you can thank me for showing you the eternal essence of your wasteful, humdrum life.

Each time you sleep, find comfort in my grin and peeping eyes,

About Author

Gitte Tamar

Brigitte, "Gitte," Tamar was born in a small rural Oregon town. Growing up, she was enthralled by scary tales featuring poetic tones and consistently gravitated towards writing darkened narratives. In the different story-lines, Brigitte explores the harsh realities of social issues faced by today's generations. This includes the dark outcomes brought on by peer pressure, addiction, homelessness, mental illness, childhood trauma, and abuse. She feels it is essential to share narratives that refrain from sugarcoating the topics society tends to shy away from.

www.ingramcontent.com/pod-product-compliance
Lightning Source LLC
Chambersburg PA
CBHW050832190726
48286CB00007B/2053